Hidden Strangers

OTHER TITLES BY MINKA KENT

After Dark

Gone Again

The Silent Woman

Unmissing

The Watcher Girl

The Trophy Wife

When I Was You

You Have to Believe Me

The Stillwater Girls

The Thinnest Air

The Perfect Roommate

The Memory Watcher

Dangerous Strangers Thrillers

Circle of Strangers

Imaginary Strangers

Hidden Strangers

MINKA KENT

THOMAS & MERCER

Published by Thomas & Mercer, Seattle

www.apub.com

Amazon, the Amazon logo, and Thomas & Mercer are trademarks of Amazon.com, Inc., or its affiliates.

EU product safety contact:
Amazon Media EU S. à r.l.
38, avenue John F. Kennedy, L-1855 Luxembourg
amazonpublishing-gpsr@amazon.com

ISBN-13: 9781662527043 (paperback)
ISBN-13: 9781662527036 (digital)

Cover design by Ploy Siripant
Cover image: © Westend61 / Getty

Printed in the United States of America

For those who saw it coming—and for those who didn't.

PROLOGUE

Every house has rules. Some people make you take your shoes off at the door. Others don't allow food beyond the kitchen. There are homes where solicitors are warmly greeted as if they're company, and then there are places where the doorbell goes ignored every time. Some families are big on privacy and courtesy, while others are more focused on cleanliness.

In this house, there are rules for survival.

Like don't ask too many questions.

Don't argue with Lucinda—ever.

Be grateful for everything, even if you didn't ask for it, or there'll be consequences.

Always act like everything is fine, even if it's not.

Keep secrets like your life depends on it—because it does.

Never forget that real monsters don't lurk in closets or under beds—some of them dress in pearls and silk, bake lemon tarts, and call themselves "Mom."

1

CAMILLE

The only thing more dangerous than where I've been is where I'm going.

I idle at the end of the cul-de-sac, two hands gripping the wheel, mind humming. The McClindon estate sprawls across the bend like something out of *Architectural Digest*—three stories of red brick, copper gutters, a pristine facade that glints under a late-morning sun.

It looks like a fortress, and in some ways, I hope it is.

The kids are restless behind me. Georgiana kicks the back of my seat with her sneakered foot, while Jackson sighs dramatically and presses his forehead against the window.

"Is this it?" Georgiana asks, her newly cropped hair tucked under a thrifted New York Yankees ball cap. "Is this Grandma's house?"

Grandma.

The word tastes like ash and dirt. I force my jaw to unclench before I turn to face them.

"Yes," I say with a false air of excitement, as though Lucinda is worthy of that name. "This is Grandma's."

It's the only way I could frame this that didn't involve nightmares or misunderstandings. Children need games, smiles, and gentle stories, so now the woman who raised me on cruelty, preyed on innocent minds, and could gut you with a smile . . . is *Grandma.*

"Remember what I told you," I say.

Jack lifts his head, his makeshift ponytail bobbing, the elastic struggling to hold. He tugs at his glittery My Little Pony T-shirt. "About the prank?"

"Yes." I glance between them, careful to keep my tone light, conspiratorial. "We're switching things up. Georgiana, you're Georgie now and we're going to trick Grandma into thinking you're a boy. And Jackson, you're Jackie. It's just a fun game for Grandma. We'll see how long it takes her to notice. And if she never notices—" I pause for effect. "We *all* win."

Both of them light up at the word "win." Children understand victory more than they understand survival.

"What do we win?" Georgiana asks, big blue eyes wider than ever.

"It's a surprise," I tell her, grinning big. "And I can't wait for you to see. But remember, if we lose, you'll never find out."

I don't enjoy lying to them like this, but I don't have a choice. I want Lucinda to know as little as humanly possible about us. She knows I have a son and daughter—she just won't know which is which now, something that might help them in the long run should she ever try and track them down when they're older.

But for now, they're five and seven, and I need to focus on the task at hand: protecting them from their lying, blackmailing, murderous father.

I reach into the back seat, lift Georgie's ball cap, and smooth her hair, freshly hacked into a boyish cut that makes her look androgynous. She keeps brushing her fingers over the ragged edges, mourning the waist-length hair that used to fall down her back like a cascade of dark satin. Jack, with his wiry frame and sharp Prescott jawline, wears his hair in the stub of a ponytail that softens him, rounds him out. His T-shirt is a couple of sizes too big on him since it's his sister's, but it has to do for now. Overall, this illusion works well enough.

I glance at their wrists—silver AirTags disguised as cheap digital watches. My insurance policy.

"Remember, never, ever, *ever* take these off," I tell them. "No matter what. We're brand new to this area, and if one of you ever gets lost, I can find you."

The truth is darker than they need to know.

"What if it hurts when I sleep with this on?" Georgie had complained when I clasped hers yesterday.

"You'll get used to it," I'd said, voice low, final. "You don't ever take it off. Not for the bath. Not for bed. Never. Do you understand?"

They'd nodded, wide eyed, thinking it was another layer of the game. Thinking Grandma would play hide-and-seek with them and want to track their moves. They'd giggled at that. I'd smiled along, but inside, I'd made the vow I always make: If anyone touches my children, they'll never touch *anything* again.

I give them both one last once-over before catching my own reflection in the rearview mirror.

A stranger looks back at me.

My hair, once a shiny shade of chestnut and a few inches past my shoulders, is clipped into a brassy, bottle-blond pixie, tousled to hide the uneven parts. The dye kit came from a gas station convenience store in a town where no one looks too closely at anyone. It burned my scalp and made my eyes water, but it did its job. I'm officially no longer the woman plastered across television screens and Reddit threads, accused of vanishing into the night with her children.

I'm a woman trying to keep her children safe, a woman quickly running out of money, and a woman with nowhere to hide but . . . *here* . . . about to sleep under the same roof as the monster who once force-fed me raw hamburger, sang me twisted lullabies, threw away my favorite teddy bear, and psychologically tortured me every chance she got.

At seventeen, I left Lucinda and never looked back. After everything she'd done, I'd wanted to murder her. Literally. And I almost did. But I left because had I stayed, it only would've been a matter of time. On my way out the door, she promised to kill me. She was drunk but I knew better than to call her bluff.

A few years later, I changed my name from Gabrielle to Camille, met a handsome doctor, had two beautiful children, and moved our impeccable little family from windy Chicago to sunny San Diego, then to arid Phoenix—where the wheels fell off.

Turns out my husband wasn't as perfect as I thought he was.

After mistakenly believing I was having an affair, he, too, turned into a monster. It started out with him controlling my bank account and ended with him murdering our next-door neighbor so he could blackmail me into never leaving.

A couple of days ago, I made a plan, took the kids, and left.

Will's been all over the Phoenix news ever since, painting a vivid and convincing portrait of a woman suffering a mental breakdown, a woman who is a danger to herself, her children, and society.

It won't be long before the entire country is looking for us.

Everyone loves a headline about a snapped woman because women rarely snap and when we do—it's terrifying. Like watching a car accident and being unable to look away. That and the whole world wants to rescue those innocent babies from that *dangerous* woman.

If they only knew the truth—I didn't snap and those innocent babies are safer with me than they'd ever be with the handsome, blue-eyed doctor giving television interviews about a version of me that never existed.

I touch the back of my neck, feeling the shorn bristles against my palm.

"We're going to go over some rules for Grandma's house. And I need you both to listen to me because this is very important," I tell them softly. "You stay by me at all times. You eat *only* the food I give you. If anyone offers you something else, you say no thank you."

Georgie nods, solemn but confused.

Jackie frowns. "But why?"

"Because we're guests in Grandma's house and those are the things you do when you want to be a polite houseguest," I say with believable confidence.

"But what if Daddy comes back? Can we eat with him?" my daughter asks.

Her mention of Will pierces like a knife, but my smile remains. "Daddy won't be joining us on this visit. He's busy, sweetheart."

"Busy with what?"

"Work," I answer. "But don't worry. He loves and misses you both very much."

The truth—that their father is a narcissistic murderer who wouldn't think twice about using them as pawns if it meant destroying me—isn't something they need to know. Not yet. If it were up to me . . . not ever. The world would be a much better place without Will Prescott in it, but fortunately for him, I have enough self-restraint that I've got no plans to take him out of it.

Unless I'm forced to.

I pull the keys from the ignition and step out into the humid air. The McClindon house looms larger from here, every glossy window staring back like a watchful eye. I scan the property the way other mothers scan playgrounds—my eyes marking every window, every door, every possible way in or out. The cul-de-sac curls behind me. Having one entrance that also serves as an exit almost makes me feel more like a prisoner than a guest.

We walk up a pristine white sidewalk that turns into a paved path to the ominous front door—pitch black like the color of Lucinda's soul. Every hedge, flowering bush, and section of landscaping has been perfectly pruned to the nines. This house not only cost a small fortune to buy, it likely costs a small fortune to maintain—which is good because it means Lucinda has what I need most right now: money.

My heartbeat is steady, rehearsed, as ready as it'll ever be.

Before I get a chance to knock, the front door swings open.

"Camille!" Lucinda's voice is a symphony of delight, warm and honeyed, dripping with the kind of affection that once drew men into her orbit and then left them gutted. Her face glows like porcelain, framed by glossy auburn hair cut into a chic bob. Julianne Moore, if Julianne Moore had been carved from steel and venom. She's slimmer than I remember, face subtly lifted, skin stretched and smoothed until the years are gone. Facelift. No question. Ironic since she's a woman who wears a mask to begin with.

She smells like expensive perfume and lemons.

She looks like perfection itself.

For a second, I revel in the fact that she called me Camille. Over the phone, I asked that she call me Camille, but the entire way here, I was convinced she'd try and use a power move by calling me Gabrielle.

Still, I don't trust a single inch of her.

Lucinda is a necessary evil—for now.

"My sweet girl," she gushes, arms outstretched, her manicured nails gleaming ballerina pink. She presses her lips to my left cheek, then the right before turning to my children as though she's waited her whole life to cradle them in her arms. A faint yet comforting scent of melted milk chocolate cocoons us, making this moment more surreal than it already is. "And these are my *beautiful* grandchildren? My goodness. Look at the two of you. Little angels."

She ushers us inside, taking my children by their hands, her energy effusive and unyielding. This version of her feels like a stranger I've never met yet know all too well at the same time.

The foyer of the McClindon house gleams. Marble floors, sweeping double staircase, chandelier dripping crystals like ice. The place smells like a five-star hotel and money. My children gape openly. They've grown up quite comfortable in their short lives, but this place makes even Will's parents' home look like a seaside shanty.

"Come, let me show you everything," she insists. We pass through the kitchen first, where a pitcher of iced tea and a plate of warm chocolate chip cookies wait for us, the chocolate still melting. "Would you like a treat? I know you've been traveling for a while. My cookies are famous around here."

My children look to me first, thank God. I give them a terse and silent "no" with my gaze. Lucinda used to lace my food with all kinds of things. I'll be damned if I willingly allow my children to eat anything of hers without further vetting.

"We actually just ate," I say, "but thank you. That was so kind of you." Then I quickly add, "Maybe we can enjoy them later."

I remind myself I'm at Lucinda's mercy right now. I have to keep the peace. I have to wear my mask at all times, matching her fake warmth line for line. Being overly obstinate or petty isn't an option. Not when I need to keep us safe and hidden from Will.

Behind Lucinda, a man with a snow-white beard and thick-framed glasses lingers near the study door wearing a gentle grin. This must be her husband. By the looks of him, he's at least a decade older than Lucinda, with eyes that crinkle and an air of success about him. He has a presence that quietly commands respect and a forehead with worry lines that aren't too deep. I imagine he's the kind of man who's been cushioned by wealth for decades.

"Rob McClindon," he says, before coughing. Once his throat clears, he adds, "We're all so glad to have you here. Please make yourselves at home."

I'm confident that when Lucinda met him she immediately deemed him as the perfect target: rich, lonely, and inching closer to retirement by the day—the kind of man who'd do anything not to spend his final years alone, the kind of man Lucinda could play like a fiddle.

Growing up, I'd witnessed her reinvent herself a million times to snag different men—but none of them were of this caliber.

I'm impressed—but not surprised.

He seems like he'll be easy to navigate. I see him as the kind of man who's just happy to be there, someone who only speaks when they have something important to say . . . because an outspoken, opinionated, domineering man would never fall for Lucinda.

From behind him, a girl appears—my half sister, Zoey. I found photos of her on Lucinda's Facebook earlier this year. By the looks of her, she's somewhere around thirteen or fourteen. We share a similar lanky build and the same glossy brown hair and curious look behind our eyes. The idea of having a half sister is one I've yet to wrap my head around. We're strangers for now, but as I ingratiate myself into the McClindon household, we won't be strangers for long.

She wears white AirPods in her ears. Her eyes graze over each of us, lingering as if she's assessing something. She radiates the kind of teenage quietude that could be mistaken for shyness, arrogance, or something sharper.

I'm curious to know what kind of mother Lucinda has been to her, but first things first.

I meet her stare with a warm smile before outstretching my hand.

"You must be Zoey. I'm Camille," I say. "It's so lovely to meet you. I always wanted a sister."

It's a lie. I'd never want Lucinda to bring another life into this world, yet judging by the timing of everything, that's the first thing she did when I left.

Zoey's face lights as she shakes my hand and matches my warmth. "Me too. I never knew you existed until the other day."

Lucinda's jovial expression flickers off for a moment before returning, making me wonder if Zoey wasn't supposed to admit that.

Lucinda clasps her hands together and the giant emerald-cut diamond on her left ring finger shimmers in the soft kitchen light. "Should we continue the tour? We'll have plenty of time to catch up and get to know one another . . ."

"That sounds great," I say, but inside I'm cataloging everything in this mazelike mansion. The sliding doors that lead to a sparkling sapphire pool. The narrow mudroom exit near the garage. The closed double doors to Rob's study. The side door propped with a mat. Seven bedrooms. Eight bathrooms. More closets and places to hide than I can keep up with. But by the end of the day, I intend to have this entire place memorized.

Lucinda sweeps us through the house like a real estate agent showing a prized property. The kitchen gleams with marble counters, a French range, double islands, and a Sub-Zero fridge. The living room is pristine, staged as if no one actually lives here. Everything is in its place—coffee table books in coordinating colors, potted plants near windows, shiny silver picture frames showcasing their happy little family over the years. Outside, their pool glitters under the sun. My children follow behind her, quiet and awestruck and for once not asking a million questions.

Upstairs, Lucinda gestures to two freshly made guest rooms with a connecting bathroom. The beds are made with perfectly tucked corners, a plethora of fluffy pillows, and fresh flowers on all the nightstands.

"This is so beautiful, but if you don't mind, we'll be staying together," I say. "The kids don't sleep well in unfamiliar places. It's nothing personal."

Once again, Lucinda's jubilant facade falters before snapping back into place. Unclenching her jaw, she says, "Of course, Camille. Whatever makes the three of you comfortable."

At the end of the hall, mere steps from our suite, a door draws my eye. It's different than the rest. Heavy and locked, with a black metal dead bolt gleaming like a warning.

"What's in there?" I ask.

"Oh, that?" Her laugh sounds practiced, just a shade too light. "There's an apartment above the garage. We're renovating it into another guest suite—one with a kitchenette, the kind of place someone could stay long term if need be. I'd show you, but it's a bit of a mess right now."

I nod and mentally file this information away.

For the remainder of the hour that follows, we continue smiling at each other and making pleasant small talk; a mirror game of warmth and hospitality that almost feels competitive, but I continue to play along.

I have no choice.

Because deep down I'm well aware that Lucinda's kindness comes with a price . . . and I'm down to my proverbial last dime.

2

Our guest suite smells faintly of lemon polish and fresh linen. It's almost too clean. Excessively prepared. Like Lucinda scrubbed the place raw to erase whatever shadows lived here before we arrived.

Correction—she paid someone to scrub the place raw.

The kids are buzzing as they unpack, chattering about who gets which drawer, who gets the side of the bed closest to the window. Georgiana lines up her stuffed fox, Mr. Red, on one of the fluffy white pillows, careful to place him just so. She's always been my particular child. Meanwhile, Jackson dumps his socks in a drawer and calls it good, already restless.

Digging into one of our bags, I pull out a deck of Old Maid cards, shuffle them, and hand them over. "I'm going to do a little unpacking. Why don't you play for a bit?"

I let them acclimate while I tuck their clothes into neat piles myself. I don't care if their things are wrinkled or crooked; what I care about is finding any excuse I can to spend less time around Lucinda.

"Don't forget," I say, checking their wrists and tapping their AirTags. "These stay on always."

Georgiana groans. "You already told us like, a hundred times."

"And I'll probably tell you a hundred more times." I kiss the top of her head and tickle her chin. "Why don't you two play another round? I need to ask Grandma something, but for now I need you to stay here. I'll be right back."

We've already seen the inside of this place, so I make my way outside, circling the perimeter of the house and keeping my stride casual as though I'm just admiring the landscaping.

The rear of the property is expansive, private, sprawling into trimmed hedges, mature trees, and an abundance of flower beds. All of it is accented with a shimmering pool that serves as the crown jewel of the backyard. I walk slow, taking my time, scanning. The motion sensor light out front caught my eye earlier—angled toward the driveway, big and bright enough to showcase anyone approaching from the street. But the backyard? The wide, shadowed space that bleeds into the line of trees? Dark. Exposed. A blind spot. I don't see a single light out here.

Interesting.

I file it away with the rest of the details I'm collecting.

At dinner, Lucinda insists on serving the children first. She fusses over their plates, ladling mashed potatoes with theatrical care, arranging their green bean almondine like she's plating a magazine spread before selecting their pieces of roasted chicken. She doesn't even ask what they want—she just decides, smiling all the while, narrating her choices like a domestic goddess auditioning for a cooking show. She even decorates each plate with a sprig of parsley.

"Make sure you save room for dessert," she says, her voice singsong. "French silk pie from this new bakery in town. The ladies at the club have been raving about it for weeks now."

It's difficult to believe this is the same woman who once forced me to eat raw hamburger.

My stomach is tight as I rack my mind trying to come up with a reason not to let them eat this food, but when I see Zoey and Rob and Lucinda herself digging in, I exhale. Besides, the kids are famished. We ate cheap and minimally on the drive here to save money, and they could use some real food.

"Delicious dinner as always, Luce," Rob tells her, eyes crinkling as he chews. I hadn't noticed until now how pale this man is, almost as if all the blood has been permanently drained from his face. Perhaps it's the plethora of white on his head and beard. Or maybe he's naturally this fair complected. Either way, I think of the way he coughed earlier and I take note.

I shove my food around with my fork as everyone else eats, my gaze roaming. The knife block on the counter stands out under the recessed lighting. Six steak knives, handles aligned. A carving knife, long and slender. A bread knife serrated like teeth.

I memorize the positions, and think about the way the bread knife gleamed when Lucinda retrieved it earlier. It's either new or freshly sharpened.

Lucinda talks as she dotes on us like a seasoned hostess, telling polished stories about her marriage to Rob. How they met at a charity gala. How he swept her off her feet. How he insisted on buying her this property because he wanted to give her a fairy-tale happy ending. The entire time Lucinda waxes on, Rob stares at her like she hung the moon. He even has that dopey, lovesick look that men get in their eyes when they're staring at their one true love.

It makes me want to vomit.

I'd warn him if I could, but something tells me he'd never believe me.

For now, I smile and nod, asking questions to seem interested, all the while searching for inconsistencies.

Somehow there are none.

The kids eat quietly, oblivious to the oddity of all this. Their lack of bickering or complaining about what they've been served tells me they're taking this houseguest thing very seriously.

Rob sits relaxed at the end of the table, peppering in occasional remarks and funny anecdotes about Lucinda over the years. Zoey inhales her food, earbuds resting next to her plate like earrings she took off and set aside. Is this a teenager thing? To constantly tune out the world around you?

I sip water, feign amusement at their stories, and laugh at all the right times. And when I finally eat my food, it's somehow one of the most delicious meals I've had in my life.

It's a far cry from a *meat jelly sandwich.*

Later, after the house has gone still, I tuck the children into bed and sit in the quiet dark, listening to the sounds of the house.

Today went well.

Too well.

And Rob, Lucinda, and Zoey seem *too* perfect.

When the exhaustion of the day finally sinks into my bones, I kill the light and settle into bed between the children, Georgiana curled against my left side, Jackson sprawled across the foot like a guard dog. I close my eyes, but I can't sleep.

At two in the morning, I hear it.

Soft. Subtle. The faint pad of feet against hardwood.

My eyes snap open.

I hold my breath, silently climb out of bed, tiptoe across the room, and press my ear to the door.

The silence on the other side is thick, waiting.

I listen for more footsteps. A shift of weight. A breath. Anything.

I count to twenty, then thirty.

The silence remains.

I twist the knob, slow as a thief, and ease the door open. The hallway yawns, long and empty, shadows stretching long under the dimmed sconces that line the floral wallpapered walls.

Someone walked by.

I know they did.

I heard it.

But who?

With bleary eyes, I stare toward the dead bolted door at our end of the hall. On the opposite end of the hall, I glance toward Lucinda's room, then at Zoey's closed door, where a faint glow of her light leaks beneath the crack. Perhaps she's still up, but that doesn't explain why she'd walk past our room this late at night.

I close the door and climb back in bed, lying still, eyes wide open, listening for the next sound.

Because if someone is walking this hall at night, it's not for nothing.

And while everything about this house looks perfect, nothing about it feels safe.

3

I'm up before the kids. The house is quiet, except it's the kind of quiet that isn't peace but a silent alarm. My mind still echoes with the sound of those soft footsteps last night. There's no denying someone walked by our door. It was harmless. But as long as we're under this roof, my guard will be up at all times.

I gently wake the kids and bring them downstairs to feed them so I can avoid Lucinda doing so. Despite the delicious meal she made last night, my associations of her and food aren't good ones. She used to salt things that needed sugar and put sugar on things that should've been salty, then when I complained, she'd force me to clean my plate anyway—all for her own entertainment. Milk was always expired. Fruit was always rotten. Cereal, if we had it, was always stale.

The kitchen smells of freshly ground coffee. Someone's been up, but they're nowhere to be found. I find a few boxes of cereal in the pantry, all sealed. Rice Krispies, Honey Nut Cheerios, and Grape-Nuts. I pick the sweetest one so they don't complain and then I locate bowls and spoons.

There's a brand new gallon of 1 percent milk in the fridge. In fact, the entire fridge is stocked with fresh groceries, most of them sealed with expiration dates at least a week from now.

I pour milk into their Honey Nut Cheerios, but not without double-checking the seal first, twisting the cap until it cracks, reassuring myself it hasn't been tampered with.

Old habits die hard.

The kids dig in, eating like they hadn't each inhaled a gourmet dinner the night before.

My gaze lingers on the coffee. It smells divine. And having not slept last night, I could use a cup. But bringing myself to trust it requires a tremendous amount of internal reasoning.

As if on cue, Lucinda appears in the doorway in yoga pants and a pale pink zip-up, her smooth red hair slicked back into a neat low bun. She's almost ethereal, her face relaxed yet polished like she's about to shoot an athleisure campaign. She resembles a kept woman who's never known a day of stress in her life—not the abusive mother who could rarely hold a job and was served more eviction notices than she could count on both hands.

I'm guessing it's the facelift.

"I'll be gone an hour. Off to yoga." She glides past my kids, stopping to ruffle the tops of their heads. "Make yourselves at home. Should be the perfect day for swimming. Zoey can show you where the pool towels are if I'm not back."

I smile and thank her, watching her slip out the door with her mat rolled tight under her arm. I don't trust the cheer in her voice any more than I trust the way her boutique perfume lingers long after she's gone.

The TV in the family room across the way hums on low volume. I glance at it, thinking it's just background noise.

Then I see him.

Will.

Giving an interview on a national morning news show.

I do a double take.

His face fills the screen, handsome in that sculpted, too-perfect way that once made strangers fawn. His voice trembles as he pleads for the safe return of our children. His throat catches when he emphasizes the word "safe," eyes shimmering with what looks like grief.

I'm frozen, taking in his Oscar-worthy performance.

Georgie tilts her head at the sound, about to turn toward the screen, but I scramble for the remote and pause it mid-frame. Will's face is frozen, his eyes wet, but subtly dead in a way only I can see.

It's a lie. All of it. Everything about him. The things he's saying. This is exactly the kind of stuff the general public eats like candy. The bastard's taking a page out of my book—if you make someone feel something they want to feel, you're the one with the power. In this case, he's making people feel sympathetic, pleading for their help, which makes them feel like they could be heroes.

And who doesn't want to feel like a hero?

"You know what? It's so nice out, kids. Why don't we take our breakfast outside," I tell them, my voice sharp enough to cut. "We can eat poolside, like we do back home."

I slide open the glass door and usher them onto the patio with their bowls cupped carefully in their little hands until they get settled at the patio table.

"I'll be back out in a second, okay?" I tell them before returning inside. I keep my body angled so I can see them. Always. Then I hit play on the remote.

Will stares at the camera, blue eyes damp, voice breaking, but beneath it all, there's a flicker of contempt he can't quite bury. I can hear the calculation behind the cracks in his voice. The woman interviewing him goes on to say the case has gone nationwide now, which gives Will the opportunity to mention that not only is local law enforcement involved, but so are three-letter agencies. He then adds, lips trembling, that he's hired a private investigator. His mouth curls at the corner with the tiniest smirk, a sick flash of satisfaction.

He's playing to the cameras.

To the American public.

But mostly, he's playing to me.

He looks at the camera the same way he started looking at me in those final weeks before I left—like I was a chess piece he was so certain he'd cornered; a veneer of tenderness worn to mask his contempt.

I'm glued to the TV, my chest tight, my fingers white around the remote.

I don't buy any of it. Not yet. If he gets three-letter agencies or PIs involved, that makes things messy, especially since he murdered Sozi in our garage. If there's anything I've learned about my husband in the past months, it's that he hates giving away his power. Putting this case in the hands of other people means losing control.

The interviewer asks if there's anything more he'd like to say before they wrap up. Drawing in a long breath, he pinches the bridge of his nose, pausing as if to gather his thoughts before looking dead-on into the camera.

"Camille," he addresses me. "Please come home. I miss you. I love you. I forgive you. I just want our family back. I promise, if you come home, we'll figure this out. I need you. And the kids need *us*."

Earlier he was trying to scare me into coming home.

Now he's trying to guilt me.

But the thing about having an antisocial personality disorder is that manipulation tactics like that don't work on us. We don't feel much. Only primal things. And even then, it's on a spectrum.

There isn't a word that man can say to change my mind.

I know what he really is—just another monster—and the last thing I need is another one of those in my life.

I think of Will's narrative. If I had a chance to control it, I could flatten it in two seconds. There are a million holes I could poke. He might have the world as an audience, but I'm smarter than him. I can play to emotions a hundred times better than he can—and those little smirks and tells that kept slipping through? I would never.

Amateur.

I shut off the TV.

Outside, the kids laugh. For a moment it sounds normal, like a morning at home. Then I remember there's no home. Not anymore.

I can't stop yawning and my eyes are so tired they burn, so I head to the coffee maker, dump out the rest of the pot, replace the grinds, and wait for a fresh brew. I need to think, but I can't do that if I'm not eating or sleeping enough.

I still can't bring myself to rely on Lucinda's food, not entirely. Not with the way she hovers around every plate, every glass, every bite. Not the way she has everything ready, all the time. It'll be impossible to stay a step ahead of her at this rate. I don't want to believe she'd poison her husband and daughter, but then I think about Rob's coughing and his pallor.

I decide we need our own supplies—more for peace of mind than anything.

I take out my burner phone and place a grocery order—granola bars, juice boxes, cereal, powdered milk, paper bowls, plastic spoons. Dry goods we'll keep in our suite. Items I can eat late at night when my stomach is grumbling or things I can hand directly to my children without passing through Lucinda's curated kitchen.

I mark the order for pickup. There'll be no going inside, no wandering aisles where eyes linger too long or a child's unexpected tantrum can draw curious gazes.

An hour later, I've loaded the kids into the car, windows cracked, the two of them singing Disney songs at the tops of their lungs in the back seat, not a care in the world. Along the way, manicured streets blur into strip malls, convenience stores, endless Midwestern chains.

On the way back, I see it.

An Audi sedan. Black. The exact make and model of Will's.

My chest clamps. I recline the driver's seat a little more and pull down my cap, obstructing my face as best I can.

The car glides past in the opposite lane, tinted windows impossible to see through. For a second, I'm certain it's him. My skin goes cold, my palms damp against the steering wheel. Then he's gone, swallowed by traffic.

It can't be Will.

He was giving a live interview on national TV a couple of hours ago—in New York.

Still, my unease lingers like smoke.

Back at the house, I unload the groceries in our room, tucking granola bars into corners of the closet, sliding juice boxes behind stacks of towels. Emergency rations. Safety in the form of sugar and cardboard.

Later, I spot Lucinda in the kitchen preparing herself a smoothie, poised with her post-yoga glow, gliding through the kitchen without a care in the world.

In this moment, I consider telling her about Will's interview. If I could pull it up and show it to her, she of all people would agree with me that the signs are there—he's manipulating and hiding his true colors.

Over the phone a few days ago, I gave her a sob story about how we were having issues, I tried to leave him, and he became abusive in several ways. I told her I couldn't get into detail since the kids were with me. She didn't ask questions, only feigned concern. I'm guessing she didn't want to risk me changing my mind about coming here.

I open my mouth to say something, then stop.

This is a different Lucinda than the one I knew. This Lucinda pretends everything is perfect, always. If I were to bring up any number of the horrible things she did to me growing up, she'd look me straight in the face and deny it. Then she'd tuck it behind her glossy smile, sharpening it into a blade to use against me later.

I shift my demeanor instead, keeping things light and easy. "How was yoga?"

She smiles back, her eyes glittering. "Wonderful. Are you into yoga? You strike me as a Pilates girl. You always did have those long, graceful limbs."

For a moment, I recall the cruel digs she used to make as I blossomed into a teenager and started garnering attention from her random grifter boyfriends. Attention I never wanted. Attention I never asked for. Attention I was punished for. Attention that turned her emerald green with envy.

I decide against mentioning Will's interview.

I need to play dumb and nice.

She doesn't know what I am.

Or what I'm capable of.

And it's best to keep it that way for now . . . because as much as I hate to admit it, I need her now more than ever.

4

This house lives differently at night. During the daytime, it's polished, curated, a certified magazine spread or a movie set. But when the lights dim, *good nights* are exchanged, and bedroom doors close, something in the air shifts.

The kids are asleep, their breathing soft and even beside me. But I lie still, staring at the ceiling, listening to the symphony of random sounds, counting the seconds between the creaks, and focusing on the way water whooshes through various pipes as everyone washes up for bed and the place settles in for the night. I'm moments from drifting off when I hear something.

Footsteps.

Not in the hall this time—on the other side of our bedroom wall. A measured thump, then another. Slow. Weighted.

My pulse ticks, each beat faster than the one before. This is the wall that butts up to the apartment above the garage—the one you can only access via a locked door at the end of the hall.

The studio guest suite Lucinda said was too messy to show us because it was undergoing a renovation.

I slide out of bed, bare feet quiet on the plush rug under the bed. I press my ear against the wall. The footsteps pause almost immediately, like whoever's inside knows I'm listening. I wait. After a long beat of silence, I hear something shift. Like a chair scraping wood.

Another minute of quiet follows before I catch what sounds like a low sigh, then a grunt.

Undeniably male.

I stay statue still for a long time, listening harder, more intently, only the noises settle into a frustrating and unnerving silence once more.

A lifetime passes before I double-check the lock on our door and crawl back into bed, curling my body around the kids like a human barricade.

Sleep never comes.

Just before sunrise, the question has calcified into something that demands an answer.

With the kids still out cold, I sneak out of bed and tiptoe to the locked apartment door with its eerie black dead bolt.

Glancing down the hall, I listen for signs of life.

And then I slide the lock open.

Locks keep honest people out—but here, I'm not one of them.

Besides, Lucinda never explicitly stated that this space was off-limits . . . just that it was a mess.

The door swings open, creaking on its hinges, which sends a start to my heart.

It's the smell that hits me first.

Not dust or drywall or the sharp tang of paint. It doesn't smell the way a renovation should. Instead it reeks of must and sweat. Unwashed bedding. Cheap cologne. Remnants of old cigar smoke. The malodorous cocktail lingers in the air like a ghost.

The space is dim, blinds drawn. A glass of bourbon sits on a bedside table, watered down, amber diluted to a shade the color of light apple juice. Next to it, an old leather club chair is pulled close, the indentation of someone's weight still pressed into the cushion.

Someone was here a minute ago. I heard them. I can smell them.

An unmade bed against the far wall along with the lingering cologne suggests someone's living here—or staying here.

Of course Lucinda lied.

For a second, I envision a scenario where Lucinda and Will conspired to trap us here—but Will would never smoke a cigar, nor would he be caught dead wearing cheap cologne. Besides, he's impatient. He wouldn't hide or lurk. He'd confront, take the kids, have me locked up, and be on his way.

I step farther inside, my eyes darting over each and every detail—a pair of boots near the door, a leather jacket slung across the back of a chair, a pack of matches on the nightstand. Evidence of someone not just staying here but *living* here.

The place could use some updating, but as far as I can tell, there's not a tool in sight to corroborate Lucinda's renovation story.

I'm about to turn back, to slip out and close the door quietly behind me, when a hand clamps over my mouth.

Large. Calloused. Warm.

The taste of a salty palm meets my lips.

A voice, low and sharp, hisses into my ear. "Don't scream."

And for the first time in my life, I almost do.

5

The taste of his palm sends the sour sting of bile up the back of my throat. I go utterly still, not because I'm afraid—but because whoever this is, I want him to think I am. It's a language most men understand—freeze, flutter, helplessly offer him evidence of your fear, and he'll falsely believe he's the one calling the shots.

He breathes hot against my ear, the rhythm steady, not panicked, not sloppy.

"Don't scream," he tells me again, lower. His hand loosens a fraction. A sign of trust. The undersides of his fingers are dry and coarse, like those belonging to someone who does physical labor all day, has never heard of lotion before, and doesn't mind living in a locked dungeon at night.

I nod and he finally lets go.

We face each other in the dimness, two strangers both hidden under the same roof.

He reaches for a nearby lamp and clicks it on, illuminating his face with its dim glow.

He's younger than I expected. Mid-thirties, maybe. Sandy-brown hair cut close, a four-day-old beard he didn't grow because beards are fashionable, but because shaving isn't the first fire he puts out each morning. His eyes flick to the open door to the hallway, then back to me with a sweep of calculation.

"You can't be in here," he says.

"Looks like you're not supposed to be in here either," I say, adding a smile like it's a joke he's welcome to laugh at if he wants to keep this civil. I want him to think I'm harmless and defenseless—because I'm none of those things. "Are . . . are you squatting?"

He doesn't laugh and he doesn't answer my question. He just watches me. Waiting for me to show the part of myself I don't have—the panic, the gush, the submission. I offer him controlled patience with a side of naivety instead. It unsettles people when you don't give them the reaction they ordered, it throws them off their game.

"I'm not going to hurt you," he says, like bad men always say right before they do. He clearly mistakes my patience for fear. "I mean it. If you shout, she'll hear you. We don't want that."

"*She*," I repeat. "You mean . . . Lucinda?"

I study his body language, trying to determine if he's an ally or one of her henchmen.

He flinches when I say her name, but only barely.

There it is.

The break in the surface.

He's afraid of her.

And honestly, he should be.

I know that without knowing another single detail about this man.

His jaw works. "Yes."

"So . . . who are you exactly?" I let the words be lighter than the question deserves. My eyes drift, soaking in details while he decides what version of himself to sell me. Boots by the door, mud dried to the seams. A chipped mug with a ring of something black inside—coffee gone cold. A jacket slung carelessly over a chair back. A floorboard with a warp where a man's weight always lands first. The patinaed brass of a dead bolt on his side of the door—which means it can be locked from both sides . . . interesting. On the other side of the room is a different door with another dead bolt. A separate entrance and exit.

He takes a breath that sounds like the prelude to a confession. "I'm Evan."

"Evan . . . ?" I lift my brows, waiting for more.

"McClindon."

"So you're related to Rob?" I ask.

"I'm his son. By his first wife." His eyes dart again to the door, like he's listening for footsteps neither of us hear. "Lucinda's my stepmother."

I resist the urge to mutter a sarcastic *lucky you*, and instead ask, "Why are you living in here? The house has, what, seven bedrooms? And Lucinda told me this space was being renovated. She never mentioned you. Are you even supposed to be here?"

I shouldn't throw so many questions at him at once, but I don't know how much longer we'll have to talk and I need answers.

He drags a hand through his unwashed hair, his pale, wide-set eyes scanning the poorly lit space and settling on his unmade bed.

"I'm here for Zoey," he says after a lengthy pause. "To keep her safe. From Lucinda."

His gaze skims my face with an intensity that would read as intimate in any other scenario.

"Does Rob know you're here?" I ask, even though the answer might as well be written in the dust on these baseboards. "That you live over his garage like a ghost."

"My father doesn't know anything." There's a contradicting mix of wistfulness in his eyes and disdain in his voice. "And we have to keep it that way."

This is a son talking about his father like someone he once admired and now resents. His tone is too personal for someone I met ninety seconds ago, but some men get drunk on their own self-righteousness. It makes them stupid with arrogance, certain they can recruit you on sympathy alone.

If Evan only knew sympathy doesn't work on people like me, that it might as well be a foreign language I don't speak, he wouldn't waste his energy.

"So that was you I heard last night." I tip my chin to the shared wall.

"I'm used to having this end of the hallway to myself," he says. "Anyway, you shouldn't have come in here."

"Lucinda mentioned she was renovating this space into an apartment, and I happen to love home renovation projects. It's a bit of a passion of mine," I lie. "I just wanted to check it out."

His mouth twitches and he watches me with the eyes of a man who wants to be trusted, but hasn't quite earned it. Not yet. Not from me.

"Don't believe everything she says," he tells me.

I want to say *Tell me something I don't know*, but I bite my tongue.

"But I know you know that," he adds. "I know all about you, *Gabrielle*."

My heart stops hard in my chest. If he knows Lucinda well enough to know about me, I can't imagine she painted me in the best light or that he'd have any reason to want to be on my "team" despite his sentiments about not trusting Lucinda.

"What about you? Can I believe you?" I ask. No one would ever say no to a question like that, but the way he answers could be enlightening.

"That's your call to make. I'm just here to keep Zoey safe," he says, and for a second his intensity softens into something tired and sad and perhaps even real. "I'm telling you these things because of your kids. Keep them close. Don't let them out of your sight."

"That's already the plan," I say.

"Think of me as the security guard you're not supposed to know is here. If there's any kind of commotion, I'll hear it and I'll be ready to intervene. If things are quiet, just pretend I'm not here."

I'm beginning to wonder if he's got a screw or two loose, if he's some paranoid squatter that the McClindons truly have no idea exists. There's a wild look in his eyes, one that's intense and distant at the same time. And the man can't sit still for two seconds. He's squirmy, fidgety. On edge. Is he on drugs? Or is he some wild card Lucinda manipulated into some scheme? Does he have dirt on her and he's blackmailing her into having a free place to live? This could go a hundred different ways if I think about it for too long.

"Okay, security guard, was it your idea to angle the motion lights toward the driveway and leave the backyard dark?" I ask.

"The fewer things lit up, the fewer things that can see."

"See us," I say.

"It's the only way I can come and go without being noticed," he says. He points to windows on the back wall of the studio apartment. A pair of night vision binoculars sits on one of the sills—and on the table beneath it, rests a gun cleaning kit. That doesn't make me feel better about any of this. "I can see everything I need to see from here."

"If you're here to keep Zoey safe, why do you need to surveil the backyard?" I remove my eyes from the gun-cleaning kit and pretend I didn't see it.

His lips press flat, as if my question annoys him. "If you'd been around the last thirteen years, you'd get it."

I move sideways a step, closer to the bedside table, like I'm looking at the watered bourbon. He watches the way a man with a secret watches every hand in the room.

"You need to be careful," he reiterates. "If you're not, you'll get everyone hurt. If you want to keep your children safe, you have to listen to me."

"What do you think she'd do to them? Seems like she's got a pretty luxurious life. She's a calculating person . . . why would she risk giving up any of this?"

He chuffs, annoyed with my counterpoint. "Just don't ask a lot of questions. Pretend everything is normal and you're one big happy family. Play into whatever she wants. And for the love of God, don't mention you met me. That's all you have to do."

I let a beat pass so he can hear my silence for what it is: consideration, not compliance. He's still an unkempt stranger and the jury's out on whether or not he's an ally or something else altogether.

"My husband's looking for us. He's dangerous . . . more dangerous than Lucinda," I say, keeping my voice soft, almost embarrassed, the kind of tone that makes other people feel kinder. I'm embellishing, of course. Will *is* dangerous, but he's got nothing on Lucinda's cunningness. "He's not a good man when he doesn't get what he wants. I came here because I thought"—I glance at the floor, letting a hint of feigned vulnerability fill a beat of silence—"I thought it would be safer. Now you have me doubting that."

I play the part of the clueless damsel in distress because if Evan is, in fact, here to keep Zoey safe, there's a chance he'll look out for us, too.

He listens. He doesn't pry. He doesn't interrupt like men do when your pain makes them feel heroic. The perpetual fidgeting seems to have calmed down, like sympathy's moving through him in real time.

"Did he hurt you?" he asks, rubbing the back of his neck. His expression shifts so often it's impossible to keep up with him. One second he seems paranoid. The next he seems compassionate. One moment he seems older, weathered by life. The next he seems naive and beat down.

I'm not sure what to make of him, so for now I'll err on the side of caution.

Besides, if I'm being honest, I don't trust anyone. Never fully have—except Will.

And look where that got me.

"He hurt me in the kind of ways that don't bruise," I say, because it is true and because it sounds like something a woman would whisper to a stranger in a dark room when she needs him to choose a side.

His jaw ticks.

"He'll come after you," he says. "They always do."

"He's trying."

"I'm sorry you have to deal with that." His apology sounds sincere enough.

"So why are you really here? You don't trust your father to keep Zoey safe?" I ask.

His eyes flash. I've hit one of the live wires.

"I'm here because I know what Lucinda is," he says, voice low. "And my father does not."

"You really think she'd hurt Zoey?" I ask.

"She already has," he says. "Many times. All little things. But I've seen her do . . . *strange things* . . . when she didn't think anyone was around. And I've heard the conversations she has with Zoey when it's just the two of them. The things she says . . . no mother should talk to their child that way."

Evan's voice tapers into silence, and the pained look in his eyes tells me he doesn't intend to elaborate.

He doesn't need to.

I let that align with what I already know—what I've already lived.

"Can I trust your father?" I think of the gentle-eyed man at the end of the dinner table who always smiles like he's posing for a picture. "He's been kind to us so far."

"He's kind to everyone he doesn't have to deal with for very long," Evan says. "He's nice in small doses."

That's disappointing to hear, but on the other hand, these two are no longer in each other's lives, and Evan could easily be painting him in a biased light.

"How long have you two been estranged?" I ask.

"Since Zoey was a couple of years old. I brought up some concerns I had about Lucinda and he wrote me off. Just like that. Didn't hesitate. Took me out of his will and everything. Told me I was dead to him. That he had a new family."

"So you threw Lucinda under the bus, yet she lets you live here?" I swallow the incredulous tone creeping up the back of my throat.

"It's complicated."

I tilt my head, weighing him. He reads as sincere in flashes, like a man who wants to be the hero so badly he'll manufacture a crisis to solve. I could use a man like that.

But I could also die because of one.

"Do you think Zoey's still in danger? She seems like a happy kid," I say.

He looks toward the wall like he could see through it and into her room from here. His mouth flattens. "Looks can be deceiving, especially around here."

"Yeah. I've noticed."

"Lucinda's . . . calmed down in recent years," he adds, carefully choosing his words. "I think because she knows I'm here. So yeah, Zoey's safe for now."

"I'll keep her safe, too." Survival means learning the rules and playing to your audience. "As long as I'm here. I'm not sure how long that'll be, but I'll help you. She's my sister, too."

And I mean it—I don't know Zoey, but she *is* my half sister, and she's a kid, and I'll be damned if I let Lucinda continue to do to Zoey the same things she did to me.

I shift toward the nightstand where his matte-black pistol lies casually beside a box of matches and an ashtray filled with cigar stubs, the weight of it all denting the cheap varnish. The slide of the gun is locked forward, magazine seated. Safety on. The leather holster beside it has the look of a thing that's warmed to the shape of his spine. Paranoid? Protective? Both?

He follows my gaze, and he doesn't move to cover it. Some men hide their weapons because they don't want you to know who they are; other men leave them where you can see for the exact opposite reason.

"Protection?" I ask.

"Insurance."

"You still haven't told me why she lets you live here." If I were the betting type, I'd put money on him being her pawn. No one in their right mind would choose to live this close to Lucinda, not after knowing what they know about her. I want to believe his story about keeping Zoey safe . . . I just can't. Not yet. Something doesn't quite add up.

Down the hall somewhere the house sighs—pipes settling or footfalls you only hear when you're listening for them. His shifty gaze darts toward the door.

"You should go," he says, ushering me closer to the hallway. "If she wakes up and sees this door open, it's not going to be good for either of us."

"She's probably at yoga," I say, teasing a bit to garner a bit of camaraderie while I have the chance. "She won't sweat if she can't photograph it and put it on Facebook."

"If you stay," he says, my attempt to build a rapport falling on deaf ears, "you follow my rules like they're law. You do what she says. You lock your door at night. You don't ask questions deeper than surface level. Do whatever it takes to stay on her good side."

"I've been practicing since I was a kid," I say. Not that staying on her good side ever worked, but I'm not about to risk being on her bad side all over again. Unfortunately I'm in too vulnerable a position to do that.

"I know," he says, and for a second I think he's going to say something more. Instead he glances at the gun, then at me. "If Lucinda mentions me—and I don't think she will—but if she does . . . don't believe a word she says. Promise me that."

I let that hang in the air for a beat. It's a concerning thing to say.

"Noted." I move past him, close enough to feel the heat rising off his shoulder. He doesn't touch me again, but I feel the ghost of his hand the way your skin remembers a sunburn after the sun is gone.

I slip into the hall and pull the door shut, turning the dead bolt with a gentle precision that makes almost no sound. The corridor is empty in that staged way, every runner perfectly spaced apart and aligned, every framed photograph sparkling and polished. Every sconce glowing dust-free. I return to our room where the kids are beginning to stir.

The silver AirTags on their wrists shine when the light hits, little full moons that promise me a location but don't guarantee a heartbeat. I smooth the top quilt with the practiced hand of someone about to get comfortable and sleep with one eye open.

That's when I see it.

Sticking out from under my pillow is a white folded square of lined paper, small enough to disappear under a palm. My throat tightens, something colder pooling under my ribs.

I unfold it.

You're not safe here

No period. The handwriting is neat and nondescript, like someone intentionally used handwriting different than their own.

There's no way of knowing who put it here. It couldn't have been Evan—I was just with him. Between Rob, Zoey, and Lucinda . . . my money's on the latter. It reeks of her signature mind games. She always loved to keep me scared. It was her favorite pastime.

I fold the paper back up and slide it into the pillowcase where my cheek will rest on it tonight. A reminder her silly attempts to rattle me might have worked on a child, but they no longer work on a grown woman. If anything, it reaffirms all the things I already knew—Lucinda might look like a different person, but inside, she's exactly the same.

Unable to shut my mind off, I walk to the window and look down into the yard at the deep, dark stretch of grass the motion sensors ignore.

In the daylight, the exterior looks like a photograph—flawless, curated, still. The kind of place people point at, admire, and daydream of how perfect life would be here.

Looks are always deceiving.

Behind me, Georgie rolls in her sleep and murmurs my name. I go to her, press a kiss to the top of her warm head, and silently make a solemn vow: *There's nothing I won't do to keep you safe.*

Then I sit on the edge of the bed and recite Evan's rules, one by one: lock the door every night, don't ask questions, lie beautifully, keep the kids close . . .

A car passes outside, a low engine purring, then fading. My skin prickles as I remember Evan's warning: *He'll come after you. They always do.*

I fold my hands in my lap and wait for the house to tell me the next truth.

We've been here two nights and already these walls are brimming with lies.

6

The storm breaks shortly past ten tonight, a low growl at first, then the sky tearing itself apart with jagged white flashes that leave the bones of the house trembling. Rain pelts the windows in furious sheets, water coursing down the glass like the house is being scrubbed raw. The kids are asleep on either side of me, their small bodies twitching with the unsettled dreams thunder tends to stir. I lie still, awake, counting the seconds between the flashes and the booms—it's something neutral to do and gives my mind a break from thinking about Lucinda. Plus with what little sleep I've been getting, I sometimes have moments that feel like a sort of strange delirium.

I've always liked storms—nature reminding us it's in charge—but here, wrapped in Lucinda's curated perfection, even the storm feels staged, a backdrop for the theater performance she never stops directing.

The lamps flicker before the whole room goes pitch black.

A few minutes later, the bedroom door creaks.

Standing in the frame is a Zoey-shaped shadow, one hand lifted, something small clutched in her skinny fingers. For a beat she just looks at me, eyes shiny in the dark, expression unreadable. Thunder shakes the house again and she steps forward, holding the object out toward me.

It's a flashlight.

Black plastic, small enough to fit a child's hand, the kind of flashlight you'd use if you were fixing a garbage disposal in a tight space. I can't imagine it could light up more than a few feet of space at full brightness.

"Mom said to give you this." Her voice is casual and helpful, but there's something off in the way she lingers in the doorway, AirPods jammed in her ears like the permanent fixtures they seem to be. She doesn't move to leave right away. She just stands there, framed, scanning our bedroom while the storm plays on outside her like an eerie symphony.

"Thanks." I click the flashlight on, the beam sharp across the ceiling and brighter than I expected. "I appreciate it."

She shrugs, one shoulder lifting. Then she just stands, staring. Unmoving. "Candles are in the hall closet by the kitchen. I'm not supposed to touch them, but Mom said to let you know they were there. I don't know where the matches are, though."

Her comment that she's not supposed to touch them and doesn't know where the matches are catches me off guard. Does Lucinda not trust Zoey with them? She's thirteen . . . not six.

I study my half sister. Hair damp and stringy from her evening shower. Oversized T-shirt clinging to her lithe frame. AirPods in. Knowing eyes that reflect the flashes of lightning that sneak through the curtains every so often. In this light, in this context, the entire vision of her is unsettling.

I remind myself she's a kid and so far she's been nothing but kind and helpful.

I force a smile, tilt my head. "What are you listening to? Can't help but notice you're always wearing those. Whatever it is, it must be good."

The corner of her mouth lifts into something that's not quite a smile, like she's embarrassed or I've asked something deeply personal. "I doubt it's anything you've ever heard of."

I let out a soft, sisterly laugh. "You're probably right. I don't have a lot of time to listen to much of anything with these two."

I nod toward the kids who are miraculously still sleeping.

"It's just a podcast I like. Anyway." Yawning, she mutters a sleepy "Good night," adjusts her earbuds, lingers for another moment too long, then disappears from view like a ghost.

I get back into bed, and the kids stir beside me, Georgiana curling closer into my side. Jackson kicks the blanket off his legs. I smooth it back over him with steady hands, masking the chill that creeps through me when I think of the way Zoey lingered in the doorway. The knowingness in her eyes. Was she helping me—or analyzing me? Perhaps it was curiosity, like she was searching for signs we have more in common than half of our DNA.

Regardless, I have to wonder about the things Evan witnessed between Lucinda and Zoey.

But what I can do? Imagine them.

7

Late Saturday afternoon drapes the backyard in a warm, dreamy light that makes even Lucinda's perfect life look legit. The pool water is liquid crystal and filtered to within an inch of its life, and the kids move through it like sleek river otters in their head-to-toe rash guards—neutral colors, no frills, no gender giveaways.

Georgiana pops up near the steps with a triumphant gasp and slicks her short hair back with both hands; Jackson paddles slow circles with his chin just above the surface, long lashes clumped with water, the stubby ponytail at the nape of his neck dark as kelp. If anyone were watching from a distance, they'd just see two kids in unremarkably neutral swim gear.

I sit at the pool's edge with my calves in the water and a plastic tumbler Lucinda pressed into my hand in the kitchen earlier, claiming it was the ideal poolside cocktail—crisp and refreshing. I accepted it with the grace of a daughter whose mother had never once forced her to drink spoiled milk or told her the purple water in her cup was Kool-Aid and not paintbrush water. The moment she stepped away, I poured the contents into the sink and refilled it with water from the tap.

Across the lawn, the garage apartment looms at the edge of the property like a thought you can't stop thinking once you've had it. One of the blinds on the attic's small window is tilted askew—a single slat off angle. Evan's been watching. Every few minutes I swear I see the faintest slip of shadow crossing behind it, and I think of the shifty man who claims he's living there for the sole purpose of keeping Zoey safe.

Lucinda and Zoey join us after a while, Lucinda opting to lounge nearby in a chaise under a striped umbrella, ankles crossed, tortoiseshell designer sunglasses oversized with lenses shiny enough to double as a mirror. A paperback is splayed on her lap but she isn't reading so much as using it as a prop, which makes sense because I've never seen her read a book in her life.

She glances over as if to check on us before tilting her head toward the garage apartment window for a fraction of a second. No one notices—except me.

Zoey floats on her back, drifting along the coping like a boat lost at sea, observing the kids play with mild amusement. For once, her AirPods aren't in, but they're resting on the ledge of the pool.

Funny how she never lets those things out of her sight.

Rob appears for a moment in the kitchen's sliding glass doors with a glass of pale beer and then disappears again, as if he changed his mind about joining us. I want to believe he's as nice as he seems, that he's not the jerk Evan made him out to be, but only time reveals that sort of thing, and I don't plan to be around long enough to find out.

"Ten more minutes, kids," I call, cheerful, maternal. "Then we're done swimming for the day."

The splashing water muffles their acknowledgment into bubbles.

Zoey floats closer to the kids, as if she wants to interact with them but isn't sure if they'd want to play with her. They've been unusually shy around her since we got here, and she's got a sort of oddness about her that only children sometimes have. I suspect they're all just feeling out of sorts and trying to make sense of several things that likely confuse their little minds. With enough time they'll warm up to one another, but my hope is we'll be out of Zoey's hair by then.

I still need to warm Lucinda up enough to get to the point I can ask her for money . . .

What little cash I have left won't get us far. Staying here is just a lily pad to buy us time and keep us from burning through our funds. Had I taken us to a women's shelter, someone would've spotted us on the news and turned us in immediately. Motels add up. Airbnbs are too expensive. And Will would never think to find me here. He knows all about the horrid things Lucinda did to me as a child. He knows she's the sole reason I changed my name and entire identity. He knows everything I've ever done was to protect our kids from her. This is truly the last place he'd think to look for me—which is also why I don't buy the whole private investigator or three-letter agency thing. Will wouldn't look for me here, but someone who finds missing people for a living would.

If I'm wrong, though, we're on borrowed time—which means I have to figure out a way to ask Lucinda for money. If I ask too soon, she'll feel used. Understandably. Because I am using her. But I could see her being vindictive, telling me she'll grab some cash next time she's at the bank and then finding a million excuses to delay it. She wants to keep me here . . . as punishment for leaving her.

"Mom, watch!" Georgiana pushes off the wall and glides underwater to my ankles. A moment later, two little hands grip my shins and a face emerges, triumphant. I clap. I praise. I trade a smile with Lucinda when she glances over wearing an adoring, pride-filled grin, acting like the kind of mother she probably pretends to be at brunch with the other "club" ladies.

She studies me hard. I feel it. Even with her giant sunglasses disguising her eyes.

It's then that I wonder if she's silently seething with jealousy inside, hating that I'm the kind of mother she never could be. Sometimes I'm certain she hated me the second I came out of her body.

Lucinda's tells have always been small: a pause that fits inside a breath, a single muscle at the jaw that tightens then releases—a metronome of counterfeit grace.

I shade my eyes with my hand and look past the kids to the attic window. There it is again, the slat moving, the angled eye adjusting.

I need to talk to Evan again.

I don't think he was lying about his relationship with Lucinda being complicated because everything with her is always complicated. But I need details and context . . . especially if he's sleeping with a gun on his nightstand, mere steps away from my children and me.

"You know, the other night, I thought I heard something on the other side of the bedroom wall." I angle toward her. "Is anyone staying in the apartment above the garage? A contractor maybe?"

Lucinda freezes for less than a second before the freeze softens into an overdone laugh, as if I've told the funniest story about a neighbor's dog.

"Goodness, no." She slides off her sunglasses and cleans a lens with the corner of her swimsuit cover-up. "It's a disaster up there. Not remotely livable. The last guy we hired half finished the drywall and then up and left. Cashed the check, too. Very frustrating. Haven't had time to find a new guy but it's on our to-do list."

She slips the glasses back on and tips her head, her smile returning to its assigned place.

"Ah, okay. I swore I heard footsteps last night," I insist—lightly. I don't want to ruffle feathers, but I also don't want to give her any reason to think I'm gullible.

"This house was built in 1932. It's almost a century old. Always expanding and contracting with the weather. Doors shift. Pipes clank. Floors creak. Wouldn't surprise me if we had some paranormal roommates in the mix." She chuckles, leaning in like she's about to divulge a secret. "But don't tell Zoey I said that. She won't sleep for weeks. Poor thing is *terrified* of ghosts."

Zoey's eyes hitch toward us, quick, then away. I can't know for sure if she heard us, but I'd bet money Lucinda tortured her with ghost stories when she was younger.

"Thought maybe you'd tucked a college kid up there," I say. "Nanny suite. Exchange student. Live-in help for those days when yoga runs long."

This time her laugh is closer to a cough. "God, no. I hate having strangers in my house."

Lucinda's statement launches effortlessly off her tongue, but the undercurrent of her words hits hard.

She knew exactly what she was saying.

We're strangers.

And we're in her house.

She reaches for the pitcher beside her, rising to refill my tumbler without asking. She pours the stream slowly, pretending to do it with care, like she wants me to feel like she's doting on me.

"Anyway," she says, and the word is a clean pivot, "Zoey's piano recital is next week. We'd love if you and the kids would join us. We'll need to find something appropriate for you to wear. You've always looked so lovely in navy. I might have a dress you could borrow. It's a little big on me." She studies me with squinted eyes behind her oversized sunglasses. "Have you thought about letting your hair grow out? This cut is . . . daring."

"I appreciate the invitation, but we have to lay low." I smile at my drink and don't bring it to my mouth, ignoring all the passive-aggressiveness she just hurled at me like a grenade. "And my hair will grow."

"I've got the best stylist in town," she says before grimacing. "I could make you an appointment. Maybe he could . . . clean it up a bit?"

I'm well aware it looks awful. I did it myself in the bathroom mirror of a roadside motel room with a pair of scissors I bought at the Dollar Tree. How it looked was the least of my concerns. It was going to be shoved under a ball cap most of the time anyway.

The kids splash. A neighbor dog barks; the sound wobbles over the fence like a drunk uncle, out of place in this curated silence. A bee drowns in the shallow end and spins in small, frantic circles. Zoey takes a video of it and taps the screen twice to focus, her nails short and clean, her hands steady like someone who doesn't flinch at suffering because perhaps to her, it's normal.

"Mom," Jackson says, "watch me."

I watch him again and let my eyes be the soft place my children land so I can keep the rest of me hard where it matters.

Lucinda takes a seat beside me, dipping her feet in the water, moving closer, almost conspiratorial. "I hope you know you three are welcome to stay as long as you'd like. You could really settle here, you know. We have room, we have everything you could need, and the children have so much fun in the pool. Not to mention our school district is one of the top in the state, but if you wanted to go the private route, Rob and I know people who could get you into a couple places."

I can barely afford granola bars, let alone private school tuition.

"That's all very generous," I say, flattery intentional. I know better than to turn down her offer right now. It's too soon to rock the boat. I need to be easy, compliant. "With everything going on, it *would* be nice to feel . . . safe." I swallow the word like a pill. "And fall will be here soon. I need to sign the kids up for school. If we stayed, I could even help manage the renovation . . . if you want the apartment usable sooner."

I mean none of that last part, but I want her to think that I do so that when I finally ask her for money, maybe she won't think I've got one foot out the door.

"Well, we wouldn't expect that, but the offer is certainly tempting." She sips her drink, one poured from the same pitcher, and I seek refuge in the fact that it likely isn't poisoned. "Zoey, my love, no phones near the water. If you drop it again, I'm not replacing it this time."

Zoey doesn't answer. I bet Lucinda's burning on the inside at the disrespect, conspiring about how she'll make her pay later.

I hope I'm wrong.

I decide to divert Lucinda's focus away from Zoey, who's doing nothing but being a typical teenager.

"Do you still keep the spare keys in the old rooster cookie jar?" I ask, like I'm remembering childhood, like I'm playing with nostalgia because nostalgia and rewriting history are how people tell themselves they're safe in spaces they once were not.

"Oh goodness," she says, a french-manicured hand splayed on her décolletage. "I forgot all about that old cookie jar. I can't believe you remember it."

How could I not? She used to hide other things in there, things she wanted me to reach my hand into and retrieve instead of keys. I'll never forget the time I pulled out a dead, bloated mouse.

"You've been such a good host, and I can't thank you enough for that. The kids are having the best time here already. I'd love if you'd let me make dinner as a way to show my appreciation," I offer. "You can relax and put your feet up. I'll take care of everything and clean up the mess, too."

"What a thoughtful suggestion," she says, and this time I feel like she means it, because being doted on reiterates how important and special she believes she is. She stands, stretches like a cat, and resettles her cover-up so that it falls just so. "But only if I can do the dessert. I make a lemon tart so good it'll make you cry." Her fingertips graze my shoulder delicately. "In a good way."

The touch combined with her words give me chills.

Everything with her is doublespeak. Always.

"I look forward to it," I lie through my teeth.

The sun slides lower and the day tips toward the hour when the yard goes from dreamy to haunted by the ghost of a man hiding above the garage. A man with a gun. A man who told me to keep my kids close and not ask any questions. A resident Lucinda vehemently denies exists and mysteriously allows to live here.

A cool breeze rustles the trees.

"Mommy, I'm cold," Jackson announces, teeth chattering for effect. "It's fr-fr-freezing."

"Okay, out," I say. "Both of you. Towels. Shoes. We're going to wash up for dinner. You want to help me make some spaghetti?"

They seem excited at the idea, shivering as I wrap them tight as burritos and kiss their rosy cheeks for anyone who is watching and for them. They need some kind of normalcy in this strange new world I've subjected them to.

Zoey climbs out of the pool, wrapping an oversized cabana towel around her lissome frame.

Lucinda rises from her lounger, stretches again, and smooths a hand down her sleek hair.

"I'm feeling a bit famished. I forgot to eat lunch earlier. Silly me. Camille, would you start the water for the pasta? There are pots in the drawer to the left of the stove. There should be a loaf of French bread in the pantry, too, if you'd be so kind as to make some garlic bread." She looks back at me, one brow higher than the other. She enjoys ordering me around like the help. "The big knives are in the block. The little ones are in the drawer." Her chin tilts. "We keep them very sharp, so please be careful."

The sharp knife comment lands like a subtle threat.

"Of course," I say. "Garlic bread sounds perfect. I can even make a salad."

She grins wider than ever. "It truly is nice having you here. I hope you know that. I'm excited for our next chapter. It's long overdue."

With those words, the air turns ten degrees colder.

What, exactly, is long overdue? It certainly isn't repairing a bond that was never there to begin with.

Lucinda glides toward the house, her bare feet silent on the stone pavers. Zoey follows, slow as syrup, one earbud out now, half listening to the sky. At the threshold, Zoey looks over her shoulder and meets my eyes directly. It's brief, unblinking, unsmiling. Then she disappears inside, swallowed by chilled air, lemon polish, and a mother who wears her persona like a costume.

I shepherd my kids inside, towel them again, and set them up at the counter with markers and pieces of paper torn from a notebook I find in the junk drawer. I stand at the stove and locate the correct pot on the first try because I already inventoried while pretending to admire the tile earlier.

"You sure know your way around a kitchen," Lucinda says while she watches me prepare dinner. If she had a tail she'd be swishing it. "How'd you learn?"

I'm unsure how to respond. If I tell her I taught myself, she'll take that as the dig that it is. If I tell her I learned from the best, she'll know I'm lying. If I mention my mother-in-law, she'll get jealous and take it out on me.

It's another one of Lucinda's unwinnable games.

"Having kids helps," I say as I slice the French bread. She watches closely, and when I'm finished, I set the blade down with a gentle finality, something unthreatening.

While I boil and salt the pasta, stir, test, and drain, she begins to work on her lemon tart. In the midst of it all, I pour my drink down the sink while her back is turned and refill the tumbler with more tap water. I miss nothing and let her believe I miss everything—including the stack of graded homework on the counter. Thinking of that note under my pillow the other night, I examine Zoey's handwriting.

It isn't the same, not even close.

When dinner is done and the tart is served like sunshine on a crust, I wait for Zoey and Rob and Lucinda to dig in before following suit and nodding to the kids that they can eat their slices. Once finished, I praise it like it rescued me from a burning building.

Lucinda is tickled.

Mission accomplished.

After kitchen cleanup and feigned yawns, I take the kids upstairs and begin the choreography of pajamas and bedtime stories. Once they're out cold, I drift to the window that overlooks the front and watch the yard harden into its nocturne. The motion lights remain dark and unbothered.

Evan must come and go through the backyard, using the side door so no one sees him. Lucinda's obviously lying about the apartment being vacant—but why?

There's also the chance that she isn't lying, that she has no idea Evan's here, and that's the reason he warned me not to say anything to her, not to ask questions.

Sometimes it's safer not to know things—as much as I hate to admit it.

I lock our bedroom door and lie down between the kids like a bridge between two small, defenseless countries, staring at the ceiling while the house plays its nightly sonata of creaks and moans and ghostly footsteps.

After a bit of ruminating, I decide Evan is staying in the apartment over the garage, but only because Lucinda decided he could.

That alone should be reason enough not to trust him.

8

The kids are asleep, one curled against my ribs, the other sprawled like a starfish across the plush duvet, their skin sticky from summer sweat and sunscreen. The house has gone silent again, that curated hush Lucinda cultivates as if quiet itself were proof of her perfection. I slip my phone from beneath the pillow, brightness dimmed to the lowest setting, and let the glow bathe my face.

Holding my breath, I google my name.

The news tabs stack faster than I can read them: local coverage, national pickup, trending hashtags. Pictures of my face, pale and overexposed, stare back at me from the various unflattering photos Will provided these outlets. His voice clips are embedded in half the articles, trembling grief manufactured into sound bites of him pleading for me to bring the kids home safe, insisting "we can work through this" when we both know that's a lie. The comments sections on these articles are a cesspool of digital pitchforks.

Never did I imagine there'd come a day when I would be hated en masse by strangers.

But the real action is in an incredibly active subreddit called r/FindCamillePrescott. There's an entire forum devoted to me, to my children, to my absence, and my perceived mental unwellness. Six thousand eight hundred and five members and growing by the minute.

I scroll through threads that run hundreds of comments deep. False spottings in airports, diners, amusement parks. Redditors swearing they saw me in Ohio, in Georgia, in line at a Target in Kansas. Some posts even have photos—blurred thirtysomething women with two children, none of them me—posted by obsessed, anonymous armchair detectives.

Reading these makes me feel ahead, almost smug. Every time someone swears they saw me somewhere I wasn't, it means we're still invisible here.

I create a dummy account with a throwaway username and add some commentaries to the mix, encouraging the theories and sightings that are the most off. There's a post about seeing me at a bus stop in Detroit, two kids in tow, a man nearby with sunglasses. I write: A bus makes sense since she didn't leave with her car. A response to that comment suggests someone helped me leave. A response to *that* response states maybe I bought a different car.

In the next thread, someone writes about seeing me in a grocery store in Phoenix. I waste no time creating another dummy account and quickly typing out: She very well could still be in Phoenix, hiding in plain sight. I do this for the hour that follows, posting dozens of lies, glittering decoys for strangers to chase.

Then I make an actual post, titling it **Devil's Advocate Theory**, to which I go on to elaborate: Happy wives don't pick up and leave with their kids. She had to have felt she was in danger. Her husband gives me the creeps. He's got dead eyes and his story doesn't add up. He says he's a great husband and they had a perfect life. People don't run from perfect lives. My 2 cents? Something happened, Camille felt her kids were in danger, and she did what she had to do.

Women respond, most of them swooning over his jawline, his posture at the podium, his perfectly mussed hair that looks accidental but never is, the fact that he's a doctor from a prominent New England family.

The comments stack up faster than I can keep up with them:

He's just a desperate dad, stop villainizing him.

Idk if he's crazy, but he's crazy hot.

> Women snap all the time. This poor man just wants
> his kids home. His wife sounds like a nutjob.

It gives me a little thrill, throwing them off my scent, planting seeds of doubt that will eventually sprout with a little more time, controlling the narrative in my own way.

I create another account and throw a darker theory into the mix—one where I state I believe he murdered them all and he's pretending they left. I reference other cases where husbands have done this exact thing.

Replies of all varieties pile in. Some agreeing. Some not.

There's no denying the internet loves Will. And I can't blame them. He puts on a hell of a show. He's convincing. And then there's the whole halo effect phenomenon—if you're attractive or high status, people are more likely to believe you're a good person.

My thoughts veer to Lucinda for a second—this is exactly what she's doing, just at a much higher level than ever before. Yoga? Country club? Multimillion-dollar mansion ripped from the pages of a magazine? Homemade tarts and a warm, effusive, welcoming persona? Who *wouldn't* trust her?

I marinate in my own disbelief for a moment, frustrated with myself for trading one monster for another. I should've known. But then I wouldn't have Georgie and Jackson.

The Reddit comments under my last post spread like gasoline catching a spark. All of it noise, distraction, confusion, seeds of doubt planting and sprouting just as I intended. I've not been sleeping well since we got here, but I have a feeling tonight I might actually sleep like a baby.

The latest storm outside has passed, leaving only damp air and a hum of insects. Inside, the house stays silent. My children breathe beside me, tethered by the AirTags they don't realize are shackles. As my eyes grow heavy, my thumb hovers over the screen, typing more lies that sound like truths, truths that look like lies, feeding the machine that feeds on me.

If the world's going to write my story, I'm at least holding the pen.

9

When I stretch my arms beneath my pillow the next morning, my fingers catch on something hard and cold: a folded hunting knife.

The blade gleams when I snap it open, sharp enough to split flesh without effort. Beneath it lies a note, the same neat, nondescript handwriting as before pressed into four words: **to keep them safe.**

Who slipped this under my pillow while my children and I slept inches away? Did I not lock the door last night? I think of Lucinda's knife comments and the way she watched me slice the French bread at dinner last night. This is just another one of her mind games. She already knows I'm on edge, that I don't trust her and don't want to be here, that I'm at her mercy. This is the perfect way to get inside my head—her favorite place to live.

I'm not afraid of her. I don't feel fear. Instead, I focus on my strategy. Strategy keeps you alive. I retract the blade and slide the knife inside my bra, the smooth metal of its handle ice cold against my warm skin.

I'm keeping it—just in case.

It's a small knife, but it's better than nothing.

For the time being, we're stuck here.

I just hope to God I won't need to use it.

I listen to the kids' even breaths as the sun begins to rise. Georgie's fox is tucked tight under her arm.

While the house is still draped in curated silence, I slip out of bed. My plan is simple: knock on Evan's door and carefully manipulate him into telling me what's so complicated about his relationship with Lucinda.

But the instant I step into the hall, I feel a presence at the other end.

Lucinda's perfume arrives first—citrus and lilies and something exotic.

"You're up early," she greets me with a sleepy morning smile. She's dressed in a head-to-toe yoga set. Deep plum. Starch white sneakers on her feet. Slicked-back low bun. The kind of sculpted body even a college girl would envy.

Standing before me, she might as well be a stranger.

But she's a stranger I know too well.

"Thought I'd make the morning coffee before everyone got up," I lie.

She presses a manicured hand to her chest and tilts her head, as if she finds the gesture endearing. "That would be so lovely, sweetheart."

Sweetheart—this ethereal monster called me a lot of things in my younger years but never anything close to that.

I stay rooted in the hallway until she floats down the stairs, the knife still pressed against my ribs on the inside of my bra.

Making my way to the kitchen, the house teems around me, full of secrets. My mind wanders to its residents, wondering which of them thinks they're playing me—and which of them doesn't realize I've been playing them since the second I arrived.

10

Tonight's dinner is staged like an advertisement for domestic bliss. The roast glistens, bronzed to perfection, surrounded by sauteed vegetables cut into neat, even shapes. The salad shines under a gloss of vinaigrette, every leaf arranged as if the bowl were prepared for a photograph. A basket of rolls rests between two polished silver butter knives. Candles burn low on the table despite the early-evening light, their flames steady, their wax smooth as though they've only just been lit for effect.

It's too curated, too precise, the kind of dinner that exists not for eating but for presentation.

I can't imagine they eat like this every night . . . but I'm beginning to think they do.

All this appears natural for Rob and Zoey.

Evan might have been telling the truth. I could see Rob being oblivious to Lucinda's evil ways because she plays him so well when they're together.

Lucinda presides at the head of the table like a queen at court, her movements fluid and flawless. Every gesture rehearsed. She passes the potatoes with a smile that contrasts the sharpness in her eyes, then she tells a charming story about Zoey's latest school project, and interrupts herself at all the right moments with self-deprecating laughter. As always, she looks immaculate—hair smooth as glass, makeup untouched by sweat or stress, posture and presence that communicates control.

Rob sits opposite me, and it takes only one glance to see he doesn't match the scene. Despite his perma-smile, he's especially pale tonight, his skin clammy under the dining room lights, sweat beginning to bead at his hairline. His button-down dress shirt clings to him in a way that suggests a fever. The closer I look, the more I realize his smile is tight, brittle, the edges of it quivering with the effort to maintain the illusion. He reaches for his water glass more often than usual, taking small sips like a man rationing strength. His hand trembles each time he places it down.

Something's not right about him.

The children sit flanked beside me, their heads ducked, their hands moving automatically. Georgie pokes at her peas, shifting them across her plate in neat lines. Jackson eats more quickly, perhaps hoping the faster he finishes, the faster he can escape the tension that even children can pick up on. They keep darting their eyes to me as though trying to read my face, looking for answers to questions they haven't asked, questions I wish I could answer.

They're homesick.

They miss their father.

They want to go home.

I keep my own performance steady. Hands folded neatly when I'm not lifting a fork. My smile polite but not eager. My laugh soft but not shrill.

My only job is to maintain the image of the good daughter, the grateful guest, the doting mother who is just here for a visit—because that's what we're all pretending this is: a visit.

But inside, I'm cataloging *everything*.

Rob coughs, a low sound that rattles in his chest. He presses his hand against the table to steady himself, his fork slipping from his fingers and clattering onto his plate.

For a second no one moves.

Zoey reaches slowly for an AirPod, removing it from her left ear. "Dad?"

"Rob?" Lucinda's voice cracks in a way I've never heard before, sharp and high, shattering the polished calm she wears like armor. She leans forward, her knuckles white against the table edge.

He tries to wave it off, lifts his water glass and takes a shaky sip, but the motion is clumsy. The glass judders, water sloshing against the rim. His face is gray-green now, his jaw working as if he's forcing himself to swallow something bitter.

My children freeze. Georgie's spoon slips from her fingers into her lap, landing with a soft thud on her linen napkin. Jack's eyes widen, his lips parting, but he doesn't make a sound. The older they get, the more they pick up on things—something I need to give them more credit for, something I need to be more cognizant of.

Rob pushes back his chair, as though standing might steady him, but the effort only drains him faster. He staggers to his feet, his legs trembling under his weight, then, almost in slow motion, he collapses.

The sound of his body hitting the hardwood is heavy, final. His limbs are folded beneath him in a way that looks unnatural. His skin glistens with sweat, his breath ragged . . . but at least he's still breathing.

Lucinda shrieks his name, rushing to his side. "Rob! Robert, answer me!"

Her demeanor is frantic, sharp, stripped of the calm she clings to in every other moment. She fumbles at his collar, yells for someone to call for help. Her mask has yet to slip. If I didn't know her, I'd believe every ounce of the fear and urgency in her voice.

I rise with deliberation, careful not to appear too calm, but calm is all I know how to be. My eyes sweep the table, the way Rob's glass sits just inches from his limp hand. My fingers close around it as I move to the side, sliding it into the folds of my sweater in one fluid motion. It's cool against my skin, condensation dampening the fabric. No one notices. Lucinda is screaming, the kids are frozen, watching the scene unfold, and Zoey is fumbling for her phone.

"Oh, my God, Dad!" Zoey's eyes fill with tears as she dials 9-1-1. "Mom, is he going to be okay?"

"I don't know, just hurry! He's fading!" Lucinda's words tumble out in a torrent. She kneels beside Rob, pressing her fingers to his neck, shouting his name again, lightly smacking his cheeks to keep him alert.

For a moment, everything around me seems to freeze as I recall an ancient memory. Something similar happened to one of Lucinda's boyfriends when I was about ten, maybe eleven. He collapsed, though in hindsight, it was likely a drug-related issue. She sat and did nothing while he writhed on the ground before turning pale and rigid. It was as if watching the life drain from his body in real time was the most fascinating thing she'd ever seen.

Georgie clutches at my sleeve, bringing me back to reality. "Mommy, what's happening?"

I need to get them away from here, but without money, we'll have nowhere to go and I'll have no way to keep them fed.

I smooth my daughter's hair, keep my tone low, steady. "It's okay. They're coming to help him. Everything's going to be okay. Why don't we go wait in the foyer for the ambulance?"

I usher them out of the dining room.

The sirens arrive minutes later, fast but not fast enough to erase what they've seen. The EMTs burst through the front door, their bags thumping against their legs, their voices clipped and urgent. They swarm Rob, checking his pulse, lifting his limp body onto the stretcher. Their words are coded, brisk, but I catch the fragments: low blood pressure, clammy, possible cardiac arrest.

Lucinda trails after them, her voice rising above theirs, demanding to know what's wrong, insisting they do everything they can, asking if they "know who he is" as if that could possibly be the difference between them saving his life or not.

I lead the children to the study off the foyer, their small hands gripping my arm so hard I imagine they're leaving marks. Meanwhile, my heartbeat is steady, my face composed, my mind curious and absorbing every detail of this moment because all of it matters.

For some reason, I can't stop thinking about that glass of water.

Lucinda always loved to hide things in food when I was a kid. Sawdust in my soup. Aquarium rocks in my Fruity Pebbles. Why wouldn't she hide something in her wealthy husband's drink, too? Something nefarious.

Evan told me Rob changed the will after he called Lucinda out years ago. If that's true, Lucinda would be the first one to benefit from Rob's death.

When Zoey eventually joins us, her eyes are damp and bloodshot, and her phone is gripped tight in one hand while her AirPods are fisted in the other.

"This keeps happening," she says, voice so low only I can hear it. Lips barely moving. For all I know, she's talking to herself, not me.

I wait for her to elaborate, to insinuate that he's either battling an illness—or battling something insidious.

But she says nothing.

I watch it all like I'm watching a TV show play out in front of me. Detached, numb, like it isn't my problem when the reality is this is a huge problem—for Zoey and Rob, at least. And for my children who saw part of this unfold. I need to figure out what to say to them. I can't let this distraction keep me from being the kind of mother they deserve. It's not enough to protect them physically, I have to protect them emotionally, too.

The EMTs wheel Rob out, Lucinda following in a storm of perfume and panic. Zoey chases after her until Lucinda turns on her heel and directs Zoey to stay home. Zoey argues. Lucinda, crazy-eyed, says something to her. They're too far away for me to hear it, but whatever she said wiped all emotion from my half sister's face in an instant.

The sirens wail again, fading as they pull away. The house falls quiet. The children cling to me, shaking like leaves. I hate they had to witness that.

Zoey slides her earbuds in and tromps upstairs to her room, understandably sullen.

Returning to the dining room, I look it over like a detective at a crime scene, wondering if the answer lies in something Rob ate or drank, in the house itself, or in the occupants who call it home.

11

Lucinda returns from the hospital late, the night stretching long and heavy before she finally arrives. I hear the garage door first, the low rumble of machinery, then the smooth shut of a luxury car door, and finally, the echo of high heels across tile.

Of course Lucinda dressed to the nines to go to the hospital, still wearing her dinner attire from earlier—high heels and all, like she needs to project status at any cost.

And of course she didn't stay the night there. This version of Lucinda would never sleep on some foldout cot.

When she steps into the kitchen, I almost don't recognize her. Her hair, always polished into a sleek bob, is flat at the crown, strands falling out of place around her tight face. Her makeup, normally flawless, is smudged underneath her eyes, a faint stain of mascara pressed beneath one lash. She looks smaller somehow, deflated, but it's the kind of deflation that can be refilled the moment she decides to snap herself back into shape.

It's an act. A costume. And if I didn't know her better, I'd believe all of it.

I'm at the sink, rinsing dishes I've already washed twice. The children are asleep upstairs.

For now, I want Lucinda to see me as busy, useful, and sympathetic. Had I gone to bed like it was any other night, she'd use that against me. I know it.

"How's Rob?" I ask, drying my hands on a nearby dish towel.

"How are the children?" She answers my question with a different one, and I realize this is all still a game to her. Who can be nicer? More perfect? Who cares more? Who controls the topic of conversation?

"They're asleep," I say. "They were worried, but I told them Rob was in good hands."

Her expression softens from exhaustion as she sets her quilted Chanel clutch on the counter, takes a seat on a kitchen stool, then folds her hands in her lap like she doesn't know what else to do with them. "Rob isn't well. He hasn't been for some time. He tries to hide it, but you can see the toll it's taking on him. Tonight wasn't the first spell he's had."

That's what Zoey said.

I turn from the sink, splaying the towel out to dry, letting my forehead crease with the perfect amount of concern. "Do they know what's wrong?"

Her eyes flash with something sharp, then soften again. "Not yet. He was awake when I left, and they were running all kinds of tests. But lately he's been . . . talking. About the future. About making changes." She lowers her gaze, lets it rest on her almond-shaped pink nails, her voice dropping to a whisper meant to sound vulnerable.

"Changes?"

"To the will. He wants to make sure Zoey and I are provided for," she says. "It always upsets me when he does this because it makes me think he doesn't believe he's going to pull through."

I don't believe her.

This is *exactly* what she wants.

And Evan made it sound like he'd already changed the will eleven years ago.

One of them is lying.

I tilt my head, widening my eyes just enough to convey sympathy. "That must be such a heavy thing to hear from him when all you want is hope."

"It is," she says, clutching her hands together. "He's always been a practical man, a planner, a provider. He wants to leave things in order." Her mouth tightens as she says it, though, as if practicality were an insult, as if she'd expected him to be sentimental, to say he wanted to leave it all to her out of devotion rather than duty. "He hasn't updated it in a while. I don't know what he thinks he needs to change, but I don't even want to think about it right now. I just hate when he gets like this."

Liar.

Inside, my mind ticks, arranging the information like evidence in a file.

Rob is sick.

Rob is talking about changing the will.

Lucinda wants to make certain her place is secured.

And Zoey? Was she only ever an insurance policy? A pawn? A means to an end? A way to secure Lucinda would always be provided for come what may? Or was she a fortunate accident? Lucinda would've been pushing forty when Zoey was conceived.

I keep my voice soft. "Of course he should take care of you both, after everything you've built together. But hopefully that day is a long ways from now."

Speaking to Lucinda with compassion sends a burn of bile up the back of my throat.

I swallow it down like fire, managing to keep my expression gentle.

Her eyes meet mine, and for a moment, I worry she sees through me. But then she nods faintly, as if reassured.

She yawns, her eyelids faltering.

Even monsters need rest.

I redry another plate slowly, giving her silence to fill. Surprisingly she doesn't. She straightens her posture, smooths her blouse, reassembles her mask.

"We'll know more in the morning. For now, we should get some rest." She slides off the kitchen stool, her exhausted stare boring into mine. "I know you don't believe me. And you don't have any reason to.

But I have changed, *Gabrielle*. I'm not who I used to be. And I don't think you are either."

Her use of my birth name is intentional. I don't flinch, though. I don't allow it to affect me. I don't give her what she wants. I smile delicately, nod, and wish her good night as she shuffles by, her hand lingering on my shoulder in passing the way a loving mother might do.

The touch means nothing.

Later, when the house has gone quiet again and the children are still sleeping, I pace the en suite bathroom, stopping every so often to press my ear against the wall to listen for signs of Evan, but even the house creaks seem to be on vacation tonight.

I step into the hallway to listen next, until I see it: a strip of light glowing from downstairs.

I tiptoe to the top of the staircase, my bare feet silent on the runner, and lean over the railing just enough to peer down below.

The light's on in Rob's study.

Slowly, I make my way down and find Zoey sitting at his desk, rifling through drawers.

She moves with unsettling precision. Not frantic, not careless. Like she knows what she's looking for and where to look. She slides one drawer open, scans quickly, then shuts it. Opens another, her fingers moving over papers, files, and pens. Her AirPods are jammed in her ears, drowning out any sounds I might accidentally make.

I linger a few paces away from the doorway, half in the shadows, watching. She doesn't notice me at first. Once she does, her head lifts slowly and her eyes lock onto mine.

We hold each other's gaze.

There's no startle in hers, no guilt.

Zoey doesn't behave like someone with their hand caught in the cookie jar.

She closes the drawer gently, deliberately, and without breaking eye contact, she picks up a pen from the desk.

She holds it up between two fingers. "Just needed this."

At midnight?

Her tone is casual, but her eyes stay fixed on mine, daring me to question it.

I shrug and pretend to be amused. "A pen, huh? Could've asked me. I would've found you one."

Her lips curve into something like a thin smile. "I miss my dad. I wanted to use one of his. These are his favorites. He orders them from some place in France."

Walking toward me, she opens her palm and presents an expensive-looking fountain pen, the kind with deep, dark ink, a glass body, and metal accents that very well could be 24K gold.

With that, she slips the pen into her pocket, turns, and disappears up the staircase, into the dark like she's just another ghost around here.

I remain in the study, the air smelling faintly of old paper, ink, and something sharper—an edge I can't place.

I glance at the desk, the drawers she touched, the chair pushed slightly askew.

I stand still, replaying the night in my mind—Lucinda's careful planting of her motive, her performance of vulnerability, her subtle reminder that she and Zoey must be provided for. And then Zoey, silent in the study, frantically searching for a *pen* at midnight.

Inheritance dynamics. Power. Survival. None of this is about love.

It never is when Lucinda's involved.

I straighten the chair and leave the study as quiet as I found it. Back upstairs, the children breathe softly, their wrists gleaming with the AirTags I refuse to let them take off. I slip between them in bed, my hand pressed flat against the knife I've tucked beneath my pillow for the night.

I still need to find a way to get money out of Lucinda—and then I'm getting us the hell out of here.

No good can come from staying a second longer than we have to.

12

The next morning, Rob is still at the hospital. Lucinda moves through the house like a windup doll someone forgot to wind all the way, smiling too brightly, speaking too softly, arranging things that don't need arranging, feigning that she needs to stay busy to keep her mind off everything and announcing she plans to visit him later. She says this at least three times, as if her reminding us she's going to visit him makes up for the strange jubilant energy she's projecting today.

I take the children outside because sunlight is better camouflage than four walls and a thousand staged intentions. The patio stones are still moist from an early-morning rain, the air clean in that post-rinse way, leaves dampened to a deeper green. The pool gleams with its bottled-blue optimism, but we won't be swimming.

Today is chalk and bubbles and pretending the world isn't hunting us—the kids need that after what happened last night.

Georgiana draws a hopscotch grid on one of the wet stones, numbers too large for the squares she's made, chalk dust ghosting her knees. Her brother chases bubbles that shimmer like coins just out of reach, the wand leaving a wet arc across her sleeve. They laugh when one pops against my cheek. I manufacture all the right reactions and say all the right exclamations so the sound floats back to them, and in the reflective glass of the patio door I search for answers.

At first I see only the yard, our three shadows on the stone path, the hedge line turned into an evergreen wall, a sliver of the street barely visible over top.

I slowly make my way to the gate that leads to the side of the garage with the entrance to the apartment. There are no footprints in the damp grass or concrete sidewalk, no trace of Evan anywhere.

From the corner of my eye, a fourth shadow lengthens across the far end of the drive—a man-shaped figure that resolves into shoulders and a head and the arrogant posture of someone who thinks the world owes him everything.

The man strides like a man on a mission.

Like Will.

The breath in my throat goes thin.

I squint just a fraction and duck behind the gate, peering through the slats enough to angle a better view.

With his hood pulled tight around his head and his back to me, he scans the cul-de-sac, attention stopping on the little Cavalier I bought off Facebook Marketplace before we left town, the one parked several houses down.

He dips his hands in his pockets and places his weight on one foot like patience is a sport he plays to win. I use this opportunity to study his physique closer.

Broad through the shoulders, narrow at the waist.

The stance is a memory my body recognizes before my mind lets me have it.

Will always had a way of claiming space without moving, without trying. A way of leaning into stillness so hard it becomes disarming and demanding at the same time. If this *is* him, he's grown smarter, or maybe only hungrier; you don't come to your wife's psychotic mother's house unless you believe the ending belongs to you.

It's him.

It has to be.

My mouth runs dry and I trot back to the stone path.

"Hey," I call to the kids, breezy, warm, the way you call ducks with breadcrumbs. "Popsicles for breakfast. First one inside gets to pick the movie later."

"Me!" Jackson shouts, already sprinting. "Me, me, me!"

His sister laughs and bolts after, chalk scraping, bubbles flying, two little bodies full of trust running exactly where I need them to run. I herd them to the patio door like some playful shepherd. I don't look at the gate again. We head inside and let the door seal the day out and keep us in.

The lock turns under my thumb with the pressure of a prayer.

"Hands," I say, reminding myself to be gentle, motherly. Even after years of being a mom, these things don't always come easy to me. "Let me see those sticky hands."

They hold them up. I wipe chalk and bubble soap from small fingers with a damp cloth, making routine out of retreat. I seat them at the kitchen island before retrieving a box of Popsicles from the freezer, the box factory sealed.

"Here you are. You guys are great listeners, you know that?" I keep my voice bright as I'm handing them each a Bomb Pop. "I was thinking . . . maybe instead of watching a movie, we could make a fort in our room."

They cheer because kids love forts.

They don't see that I'm building a barricade and a distraction in one.

I think of the Will-shaped man outside. The shoulders are right, the height is right, the stillness is right. My thumb hovers over the emergency text I never send: 9-1-1.

What would the police do if they came? Interview him on the curb, let him reproduce that practiced, trembling voice, the ache he can conjure like a party trick? What would Lucinda do with the drama of sirens right at her door? Use it. Use me. Use the children. This woman never wastes an opportunity, and this would be a one-in-a-million chance for her to make me look like the villain she always wanted me to be.

I quiet the perseverating with a plan. If it's him, we go upstairs and we move the dresser against the door and we call no one. If he gets in the house, we go to the bathroom where I hide the kids in the linen closet and squeeze myself beneath the vanity.

If I knew I could trust Evan, I'd knock on his door and have him hide us in there, but that's too risky. If we leave, no one can see it.

No one.

The patio door catches a sliver of movement in its corner. The shadow shifts left, then forward, then into enough light that a color bleeds through—black, like that hoodie . . . and then green—the bright utilitarian green of landscaping crews with a logo'd triangular patch covering the back.

The figure's head turns and for a heartbeat his face looks like Will's—before morphing into that of a man I don't know, stringy dark hair tucked behind one ear, safety glasses perched on his cap. Hedge trimmer in hand. He isn't looking at the house. He's scanning the hedge for where to start trimming.

It's a gardener.

A small hand taps my wrist. Jackson has chalk on his knuckles again, blue dust settling into the lines like a map of rivers. "Can we do the fort now?"

"Yes, baby," I say.

We head upstairs and I set them to work with chairs and blankets and towels and pillows. They move with purpose, the way children do when you put them in charge of something with minimal rules. I stay perched by the window, peering into the backyard, then pace to the other side of the room where I have a clean view of the driveway.

In the distance, I spot a white truck with a triangle-shaped logo on the side. A second man steps out, black hoodie with a flash of green T-shirt sticking out from underneath.

He unloads a trimmer and a red plastic gas can before going back for a bin full of shears and kneepads. This is either the most convincing surveillance costume I've ever seen or two men are about to wage war on Lucinda's immaculate hedges.

One of the five garage doors opens and Lucinda's red Mercedes coupe backs out. She stops to roll her window down, motioning at some landscaping as she talks to this second guy. Then she's gone.

The bunched muscle behind my ribs eases a notch.

I pull up my phone and check for any updated articles, any new armchair detective chatter.

But it's all the same recycled misinformation.

My throat is scratchy and parched, so I tell the kids I'll be right back and to stay put.

In the kitchen, Zoey is hoovering a bowl of cereal, AirPods in per usual. I steal a glance at her phone that's playing some podcast, but the writing is too small for me to read what it is.

"Hey," I greet her with a friendly smile.

She removes one earbud, then nods at the trash can where the Bomb Pop wrappers rest on top. "Popsicles for breakfast? Wish my mom was that cool."

"I'm sure she's cool in other ways," I say, trying to keep things neutral.

"Maybe in another life," Zoey says with a tone that's somehow wistful *and* sarcastic. Her attention rails toward the backyard. She stays lost in thought for a second before her gaze returns, skirting my face as if she's reading me. I'm impressed by her awareness at thirteen. Maybe she isn't as self-absorbed as I originally thought. "I saw you guys outside earlier. When the gardeners came. You thought it was him, didn't you? Your husband."

I begin to respond, then stop. I wasn't aware Zoey knew about my situation. When Lucinda and I originally spoke, I made it clear I wanted everything to stay between us. I framed it as not wanting to burden Zoey and Rob, which was true, but also the fewer people know we're hiding, the easier it is to stay hidden.

"What exactly do you know?" I ask.

"You're married to a doctor who abused you or something and you came here with your kids to get away from him." She shovels one last spoonful of Honey Nut Cheerios into her mouth. A dribble of milk slips out the side but she catches it with the side of her index finger.

"That's all she told you?"

"Pretty much." Zoey carries her bowl and spoon to the dishwasher, placing them both inside. "I don't really talk to her unless I have to."

Her words land with a force I wasn't anticipating.

Lucinda, with her "perfect" marriage and "perfect" house, has a "perfect" daughter who wants little to do with her.

Validation blankets me like warm honey.

Outside, one of the gardeners wrestles his trimmer to life. It coughs twice and then whines into a steady snarl. Before long, the smell of cut greens and two-stroke exhaust creeps under the doorjamb, sharp, earthy, and oily. Bits of hedge spit into the air like confetti. He moves with the practiced indifference of someone who has groomed a hundred hedges for a hundred moneyed women who pay men to do what their husbands can't be bothered to do.

"She seems like a really nice mom," I bait Zoey.

Her face contorts into something that suggests my comment personally offends her.

"Key words: 'seems like.'" She rolls her eyes.

"Mothers and daughters always have complicated relationships," I bait her some more. Years ago, I learned that if you pretend you don't believe someone, they'll spill their guts about all the reasons they're right. "The teenage years are extra hard, but usually it's just a phase."

Her nose crinkles. "You didn't talk to her for like, over ten years. She obviously wasn't a good mom to you. You seriously think she's a good mom to me?"

I lift a shoulder. "I wouldn't know, but she's different than I remember. I guess I'd hoped she'd changed, that you were her chance to do it right."

Zoey huffs, and I get the sense she's about to throw a teenage tantrum and march upstairs because she thinks I'm on Lucinda's side—so I pivot.

"Can I tell you something?" I lean closer. "Sister to sister?"

Zoey's eyes light as she nods.

"You can't repeat a word of this." I keep my voice low and overenunciate every syllable.

She drags her fingers across her chest, making the shape of an *X* that means absolutely nothing to me before saying, "I swear on my life."

"Lucinda was the *worst* mother," I say. "She did a lot of really messed-up things to me."

"Like what?" Zoey scoots so close I can smell traces of sweet oat cereal on her breath.

"She once made me eat raw hamburger for dinner. She called it a meat jelly sandwich."

"When I was five, I wet the bed a lot. She made me sleep on the toilet every night for weeks until I stopped."

"She once pretended I was invisible," I say. "She had me convinced I was dead. Another time she changed my name for no reason."

"I used to be afraid of the dark," Zoey counters, "so she took all the light bulbs out of my room. She said I had to face my fears to get over them. I had nightmares for months."

"She used to sing me scary lullabies."

"She used to read me monster stories before bed."

"She threw away my favorite teddy bear—the only source of comfort I had."

With every confession, I become both lighter and angrier. Lighter because I get to share these with the one person in the world who understands what it's like. Angrier because not only did she do this to me, she did it to another innocent child, too.

"She used to read my diary to her friends," I say. "They'd laugh and make fun of the things I wrote."

"That's really messed up." Zoey props her head on her hand. "Thank God my diary is on my phone. Technology isn't exactly her strong suit. Anything I don't want her to know about . . ." Her words trail into silence, as if she's realizing she might be sharing too much.

"Anyway." I change the subject. "I'm sorry she didn't do better the second time around. You deserve better."

"So did you." Zoey's forlorn expression would break my heart right now—if my heart was capable of breaking. "I always thought, hey, at least I have my dad." Her chin tucks down and she picks at a hangnail. "Now she won't even let me visit him in the hospital."

I'm not surprised.

"She never told me who my dad was," I say. "I still don't know. Don't think I ever will. Doesn't matter now, though. He obviously didn't want to be in my life."

Her lips press flat and her eyes hold a silent apology. "Mom probably had something to do with it I'm sure."

"It sounds like your dad is doing okay, though." I attempt to comfort her. "I'm sure he'll be home soon."

Her lower lip quivers. "What if he's not? This has been happening a lot lately."

"Do you think . . ." It's going to be risky, suggesting this, but who knows when I'll have another opportunity. "Do you think our mother is behind this? Could she be making him sick?"

"I don't know." Zoey lifts a single shoulder to her ear. In this moment, she looks smaller, younger, more innocent than ever. I remind myself she's just a kid. Whatever diabolical game Lucinda's playing would likely go over her head.

She's in junior high.

She should be worrying about her social life, homework, and piano practice—not whether or not her mother is intentionally making her father ill.

Without another word, Zoey slips her AirPods back in and heads for the staircase.

Conversation over. Just like that.

I wait a beat before returning to our guest room.

"Fort inspection." I crawl under the blanket with the children, where the air smells like clean cotton and Popsicle breath. "I was thinking . . . it'd be fun if we had code words. Like if I say 'dragon,' you get under the table. If I say 'thunder,' you go to the bathroom and shut the door. If I say 'pancakes,' you stay exactly where you are and make no sound. Should we practice?"

The kids' faces illuminate at the prospect of more fun and games.

"Okay, Georgie, you go first," I say.

"Dragon," she whispers, delighted. The two of them dive under each nightstand.

"Thunder," I call out, and they tiptoe to the bathroom and back. "All right, now . . . pancakes."

They turn into statues and fight silent giggles for three heroic seconds.

I praise them as if they've won a prize because they have: We get to be safe for another day.

When they tire of being brave in code, I put on a movie as promised, one with talking animals and a song that will live in my head until the end of time. While they're distracted, I open Reddit and skim the new false sightings I seeded last night.

Phoenix blew up bigger than I expected. Two hundred sixty-five new comments. A woman swears she saw me at a Sky Harbor gate holding a boy's hand and a girl's stuffed fox—one that looks an awful lot like Georgie's Mr. Red. The comments argue themselves hoarse and I add in some new ones, sharing all the reasons I think that's definitely them. Throwing them off our scent gives me a pleasant little twist of satisfaction.

While I'm at it, I run a quick search on Sozi—the Phoenix neighbor I befriended and Will killed in an attempt to blackmail me into staying. There isn't a single article about her to be found. Then again, she wasn't close with any family and really didn't have any friends. Even the other neighbors seemed to keep their distance. She was the kind of person who was nice at surface level, but the ones who got close to her never sang her praises.

Still . . . it's odd.

What did he do with her body?

I saw it with my own eyes. The blood. The mess. I covered it with a tarp . . . and then it was just . . . gone.

The problem is neither here nor there for now, so I take a deep breath and let it go. Then I revel for a moment in the fact that it wasn't Will outside today, and I allow relief to move through me like medicine that tastes bad but works. Soon, the tension in my jaw loosens. The tendons in my neck unwind. My lungs expand deeper than they have in days.

I mistake none of this for safety.

And I don't let it rewrite the rules or fool me into letting my guard down.

The fact that it wasn't him today . . . is not a guarantee that one day it won't be.

13

Things feel . . . *off* . . . this morning.

It starts small, the way these things always do. A door that usually opens doesn't. A hallway cabinet suddenly secured with a brass lock that gleams too new against the older wood.

The study door is closed when it's remained open since the other night. At first it all feels like coincidence, an absentminded housekeeper, a quirk of the old house settling into itself. But then Lucinda begins mentioning it, dropping little explanations in that perfectly polished tone of hers.

"I don't mean to alarm you," she tells me over coffee. "But our next-door neighbor was robbed last night while no one was home. I'm taking extra precautions . . . all things considered."

There's no way to know if she's telling the truth or crafting a narrative that makes me feel even more at her mercy, more stuck, safer under her roof than anywhere else.

"I'm going to start locking more of the doors, the ones to the rooms we don't use. Some cabinets, too. I hate the look of unsightly locks, but this place is full of valuables and priceless antiques."

My breath hitches. This isn't about a burglar. This is about me not "stealing" things—which means, once again, it's not the right time to ask for money.

"Rob says we have the best security system money can buy," she tells me, gliding through the kitchen as she speaks, setting her lemon water on the counter, arranging a dish towel, her performance seamless. "But it's such a large property," she adds, smiling at me over her shoulder. "Between Rob being gone, maintenance people coming and going, deliveries throughout the day, and your . . . *situation. . .* we need to be hypervigilant, don't you think?"

I mirror her, tilting my head, smiling back. "Couldn't agree more."

Inside, I taste the lie. The locks are not for safety. They're for control. They're not for keeping people out—they're for keeping us in.

When the afternoon rolls around, Lucinda leaves to visit Rob, Zoey disappears into her room with earbuds leaking faint bass through the door, and Evan is still nowhere to be seen—or heard.

The house grows quiet, the kind that feels like permission to breathe, to not walk on eggshells for a second or two. While the kids watch cartoons in the family room, I locate a small tool kit in the kitchen junk drawer, grabbing two tension wrenches, a bobby pin, and a baseball card. And then I go to the study, kneeling at the locked double doors that were fastened when I checked a little bit ago.

They resist for a second, finally yielding with a soft, satisfying click after a little more finessing and a lot of patience. I slip inside and take in the room with quick, sweeping glances. Rob's desk, polished to a shine.

Next to a banker's lamp, a leather-bound planner is open to a page with neat columns of large figures with a plethora of zeroes. Beside it, a framed photograph of Rob and Zoey, looking like the perfect father-and-daughter duo.

The desk drawers are locked, of course, but they're not beyond me.

I crouch down and get to work—until I hear the soft pad of Zoey's footsteps overhead, growing louder as if she's heading for the top of the stairs.

I shove the tools into my pockets, rush out of the study, and close the doors behind me so gently they don't make a sound.

Zoey flounces down the stairs, oblivious.

I breathe a sigh of relief.

Zoey just might be the only true ally I'll ever have against Lucinda.

I'm finally earning her trust . . . and I can't afford to lose it.

14

I lie awake between the children, counting their breaths, noting every creak and shift of the pipes and windows and floors. It's half past eleven when I hear it—shuffling, movement coming from the apartment above the garage.

I slip from the bed, careful not to stir Georgiana and Jackson, and move through the hall on bare feet. Sconce light illuminates the footpath to his dead bolted door. I press my ear against it and am met with the sound of him muttering, low and broken, a one-sided conversation he's having with himself. Words I can't quite make out, but they don't sound good. There's more shuffling, a breath, and then the snap of a light flooding the space under the door.

Then a metallic slick sound follows—something that sounds too much like someone racking the slide of a handgun.

My back stiffens when I remember the gun on his nightstand.

What reason would he possibly have to keep it armed and ready *tonight*?

15

I wasn't going to do it.

I wasn't going to knock.

I wasn't going to ask.

But then I heard the gun.

If we're not safe tonight, I need to know.

I rap three times on the door, hold my breath, and exhale the second the lock on the other side clicks.

Evan appears in the doorway, hair disheveled and dark circles under his eyes more pronounced than ever. I bet he hasn't slept since Rob got carted off in that ambulance the other night.

"What's going on?" I fold my arms. "Tell me everything."

"I think Lucinda's killing my father," Evan says, pacing the dark and dingy apartment. "I . . . I've always thought she might. But now? Now I think she's actually going through with it."

I keep my face calm and expressionless, though my pulse flicks faster.

If Evan kills Lucinda, I wouldn't shed a tear. In fact, he'd be doing the world a favor. But it would mean losing our hiding spot—and any chance at getting some cash. Those are the sole reasons we're here at all.

"That's a strong thing to say," I whisper back, soft enough to make it sound like skepticism instead of agreement. "You can't really believe that."

He leans closer, his jaw tightening. "I don't believe it. I *know* it. She's been dosing him. Slowly. Over time. You've seen him—he's pale, weak, falling apart. That's not an accident. The man's always been a health freak. Over the last year, he turned sixty-five—but somehow looks eighty-five."

I'd have put him somewhere in between, but definitely older than sixty-five.

I let my mouth part slightly, still feigning doubt, preparing to let naivety rise in my tone. The more I pretend not to believe him, the more details he might spill. If he has any evidence or proof of anything solid, this is the best way to draw that out of him. If she's currently in the process of murdering her husband, I'm taking the kids and leaving immediately. Money or not. I know how this woman's mind works.

For all I know, the real reason she wants me here isn't for her own sick satisfaction . . . but to frame me.

"I don't know, Evan." I infuse more skepticism into my tone, subtle enough to not put him on the defensive. "They seem really happy and in love. Why would she want him gone?"

He pinches the bridge of his narrow nose in frustration, not realizing I'm drawing him out. "His money. That's all she's ever wanted from day one."

I tilt my head as though I don't quite follow. "Really? Lucinda seems more concerned with yoga and the country club than murder. You think she'd give up this cushy life? The life he provides for her? I've never seen her so happy. She—"

"I don't think she would. I *know* she would," he cuts me off, tone sharper now. "She's good at putting on a show. That's what she does. She makes you forget who she is while she slides the knife between your ribs."

I let silence hang, hoping it might force him to fill it. He didn't answer my question, he simply explained something I already know too well.

He paces some more, runs a hand through his hair, and mutters to himself before snapping his eyes back to mine. "I have to do something."

I widen my eyes, soft with disbelief, the kind that begs for more explanation. "Like *what*?"

"It's time to put an end to the poison that has ruined this family for the last thirteen years," he says, sounding like someone suffering a bout of paranoid delusion. Then softer, leaning closer, lowering his voice until I can feel his breath against my cheek. "I'm telling you this because I know you're not stupid. You notice things. I know you do. But listen to me." His expression darkens and his voice is heavy with a threat disguised as a promise. "If you let me do what I need to do, I'll keep you and your kids safe. But if you get in my way, I can't protect you."

I don't flinch, react, or speak.

This man appears unhinged.

And he has a gun.

"Are you . . . going to kill her?" I glance at the gun on the nightstand.

He runs a hand through his hair, mussing it up even more. "I'm going to have a talk with her and go from there."

"She's not worth it." I can't believe I'm talking him out of killing the one person who doesn't deserve the oxygen she takes up, but I'm thinking about my kids. I don't want them to hear a gunshot, to see a speck of blood. "You'd really spend your life in prison because Lucinda is poisoning your father? Your father who won't even speak to you?"

"I told you it's complicated."

Is it complicated?

Or is he just pissed off enough to do something crazy?

"And I told you to tell me everything."

He chuffs, wearing a half smirk that makes me think he sees me as a naive little fool. "Don't ask questions, remember?"

I remain composed, unfazed, behaving as if he's just told me the weather forecast for this weekend. The deranged look in his eyes tells me he has a plan he fully intends to execute—and now I need to focus on getting us out of here before he does.

The last thing I need is to trade one problem for another.

16

As the kids eat breakfast at the kitchen island, I scroll forums.

Six minutes ago, someone claimed they saw me in the Chicago suburbs. Not me specifically—my kids. A girl with cropped dark hair, a boy with a ponytail—the exact reversal I crafted. They describe them playing near a fence, laughing, chasing bubbles.

There's no photo, but that was us yesterday in the backyard.

My stomach pitches like I've missed a step in the dark.

The kids haven't left the house in days. Whoever posted this either saw them here, in Lucinda's private and carefully manicured backyard, or invented the sighting with details no one could've possibly had unless they live here.

The thought makes my skin crawl.

My children have been exposed.

With shaky fingers, I log into both of my dummy accounts and type out a handful of comments attempting to debunk this claim.

Zoey meanders into the kitchen, earbuds in until she pops them out one by one. She sets an empty glass by the sink, looking me up and down like she notices something's different.

"Can I take the kids swimming?" she asks, casual. "None of my friends are around today, Mom went to the hospital to see Dad, I could use something to do."

"Sure," I say, because refusing would draw suspicion. But my yes comes with conditions. "I was planning to let them swim anyway. I'll get them ready and join you."

I dress them myself, pulling rash guards over small heads, smoothing fabric against damp skin. I kiss their foreheads, press kisses like reminders into their ears.

Outside, the sun glitters off the pool. I take the chair nearest the edge, my phone in my hand, my eyes on both water and screen as Zoey gives them rides on her back, pulls them on floaties, and bats a beach ball back and forth.

Jackson and Georgie giggle as if this is the most fun they've had their entire lives.

I pull up Reddit.

Another post has gone up since I last checked. Someone says they just saw the same two kids in downtown Chicago. While the kids haven't once stepped foot in downtown Chicago, the details align too perfectly with the disguises I created.

The realization presses cold into my bones: someone has compromised us, intentionally leaving a trail of breadcrumbs for Will.

The sun overhead burns hot, but my blood runs cold.

Our "safe house" is no longer safe.

17

Rob came home this afternoon. Lucinda has him propped up against a million pillows in their room. The curtains are drawn half shut and the air is heavy with the scent of antiseptic and the faint sweetness of the flowers Lucinda insisted he needed by his bedside. On the nightstand are crumpled tissues, pill bottles, and water jugs. His breath is shallow and beneath the lamplight, his skin appears paler than ever. He almost looks worse than he did when he was carted out of here on a stretcher a few days ago.

Lucinda hovers, tending, arranging, fussing with pillows and blankets, her devotion loud enough to be heard through the walls.

I offer to bring him tea. She hesitates for a fraction too long, then relents. "That would be lovely, sweetheart. His throat's so dry from the hospital oxygen. Some jasmine tea would be perfect. It's his favorite."

I head to the kitchen to prepare the kettle and locate the tea bags. Lucinda joins me after a couple of minutes, moving with precision, as though each step is part of a ritual. After steeping a tea bag a few minutes, I hand her the cup and saucer.

"Thank you so much." She places it on the counter by a row of canisters, stopping to grab a silver spoon for sugar, only the canister she uses is a smaller one, tucked away out of sight, not meant to be seen. She measures carefully, not a pinch too much or too little. The moment the lid lifts, a faint chemical smell clings to the air. Sweet, but wrong. Sharp. When she notices me watching, she offers a nonchalant smile. "His blood sugar's a little high. We have to use the fake stuff for now. Doctor's orders."

I think of Evan and the gun, the reference to poison, the things he's inferred about Lucinda, the things I know she's capable of . . .

"Why don't you go rest? I'll take it to him," I insist.

She pauses before retrieving a silver tray for me. I carry it to his room, balancing it with both hands. When I get to the doorway of the primary suite, I find Zoey perched on the side of the bed, leaning close to her father, her mouth near his ear, her words too soft to catch.

His eyes are open, glazed but focused on her. The moment the two of them notice me, they snap apart. Zoey straightens, pocketing whatever she just said, her expression smooth and blank. Rob clears his throat, managing a smile in my direction.

Whatever they were discussing was for their ears only.

I place the tea on his nightstand, their silence leaving ripples through the air.

"Thank you so much, Camille," Rob says, his voice froggy and dry. He places a shaky hand over mine and gives it a squeeze. "I hope you and the kids aren't in a hurry to leave. I'm looking forward to getting to know you better."

In this moment, he seems genuine and harmless. Maybe that's why Lucinda targeted him. It wouldn't be hard for her to charm a lonely, gullible, wealthy older man. People like that only want the kinds of things money can't buy, and Lucinda is an opportunist of the worst variety.

"I've never seen my wife so happy," he adds with a twinkle in his eye—like it makes *him* happy that *she's* happy. I bite my tongue. If he's truly this kindhearted, she doesn't deserve him. "She's been waiting a long time for this, you know."

Whatever she's told him about our past, about why I left, I bet she gave him some glossy, well-edited version where I was a moody teenager and we had a falling out and it broke her heart.

"I appreciate you taking us in," I say as he lets my hand go. "You should probably get some rest."

"She loves you," he adds as I'm on my way out, "very much."

"I know," I lie.

The only thing Lucinda knows about love is the power that comes with the illusion of it.

18

The family room television drones in the background, Lucinda leaving it on as if the noise itself were proof of normalcy. A local anchor fills the air with her steady cadence, covering the latest turn in the ongoing spectacle of my absence. Will appears on screen, his hair just unkempt enough to read as grief, his shirt collar open, the posture of a man who hasn't slept in weeks. His voice trembles on cue as he offers a reward—substantial, generous—for any information leading to my "safe return."

I lunge for the remote, hitting mute before the kids hear their father's voice.

Lucinda shoots me a look that reads like understanding and approval, as if she wants me to think I did the right thing because it would distract me from the fact that she turned the news on intentionally.

The camera cuts to the reporter outside a police precinct, repeating what the nation already knows. According to the closed captions, they're reporting sightings in Chicago, whispers of a mother and two children fitting my description. Nothing confirmed but police are looking and they're asking the public to be on the lookout as well.

Lucinda, standing beside me and reading the captions, too, exhales under her breath. Her jaw is tight, her mouth pressed into something more brittle than her usual composure.

I tilt my head and keep my voice even. "I don't understand how this could get out. We haven't left your house . . ."

She snaps her gaze to me, bits of familiar anger flashing. "Are you suggesting *I* had something to do with this? Why would I protect you and your children . . . only to feed you to the wolves?"

Because that's exactly the kind of thing Lucinda would do . . .

Funny how she took my comment as a direct insinuation that she was behind this.

I soften, shrugging. "I'm not suggesting anything. But someone's feeding him information. Any idea who it could be?"

Her lips thin, her eyes cold. "I wish I knew. Maybe a neighbor? Maybe someone saw you and the children outside?"

The news camera shifts the view back to Will as a morning anchor asks if he believes I'm hiding on purpose, if he thinks I chose to leave him or if we were kidnapped and being held against our will somewhere. She's regurgitating some of the very theories I've posted online, theories that've made their way all over like a rumor too good not to share.

He hesitates for half a second too long, and I know that pause wasn't for them. The shift in his eyes, the flicker of something sharp beneath the facade of grief—that was for me.

"Anything is possible, but I personally believe she's unwell," he says. "I think she's in need of help, and I'm extremely concerned for the safety of my children. That said, we've received some verifiable tips lately and we're going to find them soon. Very soon."

He stares into the camera once more, more intense than ever.

And for the first time in weeks, I know without a doubt, he's closing in on us.

19

It's warmer than usual upstairs tonight. Someone adjusted the AC since Rob's been home and now no one can breathe. I crack a window to let some fresh air in. Never imagined Midwest summer humidity could feel so refreshing.

The children are asleep, curled on either side of me, their breaths syncing like a duet of innocence.

At bath time earlier, Jackson told me he talked to his father on the phone today. Kids say all kinds of crazy things, I know that, but I'd never seen him so insistent. He said we'd see Daddy soon, that he was on his way. When I asked him what phone he used, he said he didn't know, that it was white and flat—like an iPhone. It could've been anyone's. He claims it was just sitting on the kitchen table and he heard Will's voice coming through, calling out his name.

The only solace I have is that Georgie couldn't corroborate his story. She wasn't there when it happened, he said—which leads me to wonder if it was just some story he made up to comfort himself because he misses his dad.

Still, it's been haunting me ever since.

I'm wide awake, staring at the ceiling, when I hear it—a shift outside the window.

A faint crunch of grass.

I sit up slowly, kill the lamp with a quiet click. The room plunges into near total darkness. I stay still, listening. Nothing now but the hum of the double air-conditioning units, a barking dog, and the faint rattle of leaves in the breeze.

Within seconds, there's another sound, this one closer, heavier.

I slide out of the bed and move to the window, shielding myself behind the curtains, careful to keep my profile out of sight. I don't look straight out. Instead, I angle myself.

Someone's out there.

Broad shoulders, tall frame.

A silhouette etched under moonlight.

Still as stone, watching the house from the backyard—where there are no cameras or motion-sensing lights.

My heart hammers painfully hard, but my mind stays calm, the way it's been conditioned to be in the name of survival. Panic is a luxury I've never had.

From here, it looks like Will.

Every line of him is familiar, seared into me. The self-assured stance I used to find so attractive, the unwavering posture that suggested intelligence and commanded respect, the refusal to shift or twitch under pressure. Will always said doctors were trained to be calm, to compartmentalize, to know exactly how to act in the face of any threat. He was known for his bedside manner, for offering comfort and compassion to anxious patients before he put them under.

I blink and the figure is gone.

Was I imagining it?

If I wasn't, he had to have slipped between the shrubs that separate this house from the next, disappearing into the foliage as if the night swallowed him whole.

I stand there long after, staring at the empty space where I *know* I saw him.

Maybe it was that private investigator Will allegedly hired? Perhaps a true crime enthusiast who read a thread online about the kids being spotted in this area and decided to play detective.

Or hell, Evan.

Whoever it was, there's no denying if it wasn't Will, he sure looked and moved like him.

I pull away from the window and steady my breath. If it *was* Will, he had to have been scoping out the place, plotting, strategizing.

Our bags are packed but our money is thinning, shrinking with every day I wait here. Maybe not literally, but it feels that way. I need more. Soon. I can't stay much longer without becoming the very thing he wants me to be—cornered, helpless, forced to fold and give him what he wants: me behind bars, away from the only two things that matter to me.

The children stir in their sleep, and I return to bed, curling around them like a shield. My eyes stay open long into the night, because whether it was Will or not, the fact of the matter is unchanged.

I'm running out of time, money, and people to trust.

20

Morning does little to soften the edges of the night before. I keep replaying the figure outside my window—the build, the stillness, the vanishing act. Jackson's story about the phone call. My instinct tells me it was Will, but instinct might as well be delusion when you're surviving off adrenaline and minimal sleep.

The longer I sit with it, the more the doubt creeps in.

What if it wasn't Will at all? What if it was Evan? He's hidden himself here like a ghost, moving between shadows, slipping in and out via the garage, armed with weapons he doesn't bother to elaborate on. He clearly has an agenda and warned me to stay out of his way and not ask questions. Would he have done that to scare me into compliance since I was asking questions the other night?

He could easily be Lucinda's henchman. Maybe he doesn't hate her at all. Maybe he's obsessed with her, willing to do her bidding because he's another kind of easily manipulatable man and she's—now—a beautiful woman with money.

Maybe she told him to skulk outside my window in the dark, to feed details to the media, to plant rumors online about local sightings. The disguises I built for my children were too specific in those posts, yet he hasn't even met them.

Nothing makes sense except for one thing: Someone's watching us from the inside.

I perseverate more about Evan and his possible motives.

First he said he was here to protect Zoey from Lucinda. Then he said he was worried about Lucinda poisoning his father—a man he hasn't spoken to in years and has no idea he's living under the same roof.

His story doesn't add up.

It only reeks of Lucinda and her web of lies.

Zoey sits on the back steps, earbuds jammed in her ears per usual, knees pulled to her chest. The sunlight bleaches her brown hair at the ends, contrasting off her sun-kissed skin and making her look like a typical junior high schooler on summer break. Inside, the kids are coloring at the kitchen island, in my line of sight. Outside, I take a seat beside my kid sister.

"What do you know about the guy who lives upstairs?" I keep my tone casual.

Her gaze flicks to me and she removes an earbud. "What guy?"

"The one in the garage apartment," I press. "Tall, dark hair, light blue eyes. About my age. He keeps odd hours."

She shrugs, her mouth twitching like she's fighting back a smirk. "Probably a construction worker. Mom's always hiring people."

"She lets them live here?"

"How would I know?" Another shrug.

In her defense, the door is always locked and Evan knows how to come and go without being seen. It's possible she's being honest. If she opened up to me about all the other things Lucinda did, why would she hold this back?

Zoey pulls her knees tighter, resting her chin on them, appearing lost in thought for a few moments.

"No point in asking questions around here," she says. "Everyone lies anyway."

With that, she rises, sliding her one earbud back in, the faint buzz of a podcaster's voice cutting her off from me. She wanders inside, leaving me on the step with more questions than when I started.

Everyone lies. She's right.

But some lies are a gateway to the truth.

21

The cameras start to appear one by one all over the house, almost overnight, like new moles on a body you've lived in long enough to know by heart. First in the hallway by the front door, the glossy black eye mounted high, tilted down. Then on the back patio, its red light winking in the dark like it's alive.

When I ask, Lucinda gives me her most polished smile, a performance rehearsed down to the flicker of concern in her eyes. "It's for your safety, darling. For the children's safety. For all our safety. With your husband still out there, with strangers inventing sightings online, the talk of you being in the Chicago area . . . it's the right thing to do."

I nod as if reassured, though inside I taste the truth like metal. This isn't about safety. It's about control. About keeping me in place. About punishing me for walking away fourteen years ago and making me live inside her curated cage where she can torture me all over again, in new ways.

She isn't protecting me—she's imprisoning me, the way she always wanted to.

I soften my voice, tilt my head, and lean into her performance as though it were my own.

"I appreciate it. Really, I do." I pause for dramatic effect and drag in a long breath. "I know things were hard when I was younger. You were a single mom and you were doing the best you could, handling everything all on your own. No help from anyone. I used to carry so much resentment, but motherhood has changed me. It gave me a perspective I didn't have before." I let my voice catch, just slightly, coordinating it with the crocodile tears I force to well behind my eyes. "We all have regrets. I just hope you know I'm glad you're giving me a second chance. I just hate that it had to be under these circumstances."

Her mouth curves in satisfaction, like she's winning some game.

"People are allowed to change, you know," I add, letting my eyes shine with feigned sincerity. "I don't think either of us are the people we used to be."

It's a lie. She's still a monster, only now she's a monster who drives a Mercedes and wears an awful lot of Chanel.

She touches my arm, her hand warm and lingering. "You have no idea how long I've been waiting for this. I always knew you'd come back to me."

I return her smile, but inside I know. Psychopaths don't change. They can't. They adapt. They rehearse. At best, they manage their behaviors. They can control their actions, disguise their impulses, but they can't change who they are.

Lucinda will never stop being what she's always been.

The only difference is that now I'm older, wiser, and I know her tricks.

"I think we're going to have to leave soon," I force as much regret as I can into my lie. "I don't want to . . . not when we're just starting to reconnect. But it feels like Will's close. And I don't want to endanger you or Rob or Zoey . . . not when Rob's recovering. And Zoey doesn't need to be involved in any of this. She's just a kid."

I'm *this close* to asking her for money. Rob seems to be on the mend. She's aware that Will's closing in thanks to online tipsters. She and I are keeping things cordial enough. If she wants to keep playing the role of the perfect mother, she'll have no reason to tell me no.

"Nonsense. You three are safer here with me. I can promise you that." She shuts the topic down immediately before offering a warm smile with stark cold eyes. "Sweetheart, if you'll excuse me, I should check on Rob. He's due for his nighttime medication soon."

"Wait," I say. "Can I ask you something?"

"Of course."

"Jack—Jackie said she talked to Will on the phone the other night," I say. "That there was a phone just sitting out on the kitchen table and Will's voice was coming from it. He said he was coming by soon. And the other night, I swore I saw Will in the backyard."

Lucinda lets out a cackle, as if I've told her the most ridiculous joke she's ever heard.

"Darling, do you hear yourself right now?" With that, she heads upstairs, leaving me gaslit and with a promise that feels more like a prison sentence.

Leaving here isn't going to be as easy as I thought.

22

Proof of Will's proximity has been coming in fragments, but tonight they're forming a map of the inevitable. First, a thread on Reddit posted minutes after I step into the yard with the kids—one that references the turquoise shirt Georgiana is wearing.

Another post references a rumor on a local blog about a woman with two children shopping in a grocery store only a few miles away—the same place I picked up the small grocery order the other week. Lucinda was gone when I did that. She couldn't have known. Evan is constantly coming and going, but he's got eyes all over the place. Zoey's absorbed in her own world. And Rob seems oblivious most of the time—even when he's not recovering from his mystery ailment.

I lie awake, scrolling all the threads, noting the time stamps of new comments and cross-referencing them against my own movements.

Someone close to us is feeding the public this information.

I log into one of my dummy accounts and post about spotting the missing family in Rhode Island, adding details sharp enough to be believable.

"Saw her at a Greyhound station in St. Louis," I type under another account. "Two kids with her. Looked scared."

I attach a photo I've kept hidden, one from earlier this year—grainy, poorly lit, the kids playing in a park. Out of context, it looks recent. Out of context, it looks like evidence.

Next, I ask if anyone knows who Will's PI is so I can send that to him. No one replies, leading me to believe there never was a private investigator in the first place.

Within an hour, my Rhode Island thread explodes with hundreds of comments. Arguments over whether it's really me. Some say it looks staged. Some claim it's AI. Some swear it's real. The noise builds, and in that noise, I slip farther out of sight.

If Will hasn't found us yet, I'll make sure the map he's following feels more like a maze that takes him everywhere but here. Every false lead buys me another day, another hour, another chance to figure out my next move.

23

The house has a rhythm at night, and I've memorized every beat. The buzz of the air conditioners, the faint creak of the beams when the temperature dips, Lucinda's slippered steps shuffling into silence after she makes her last pass through the halls.

Tonight, though, there's another sound—heavier, cautious. I slip from the bed once the children's breaths have steadied and they're fidgeting enough I know they're deep into REM sleep.

Through the sliver of the curtain, I catch him: Evan. Moving toward the garage again. His hand grips something long, but the shadows make it impossible to tell what. He walks quickly, his head down before he vanishes into the dark.

I've never seen him arrive in a car. For all I know, he doesn't even own one. He could be anyone, coming from anywhere, vanishing into anything. It wouldn't surprise me if Zoey was being honest about not having a clue who I was talking about.

I wait until silence swallows the house again, then I head to the end of my hall and stop at the apartment entrance. My knuckles hover for a moment before I unlock the door from my side and knock, rapping lightly enough not to wake anyone else but loud enough for him to hear.

There's a pause, then the lock on his side clicks, the door drifts open, and his eyes meet mine in the narrow crack.

"What are you doing here?" His voice is low, his gaze intense.

"We need to talk," I whisper.

He glances over my shoulder, then rushes me in. The space reeks of wood polish, cigar smoke, and human sweat. A bourbon glass sits half empty on the desk. It looks and smells exactly how it always has. I'm beginning to wonder if he actually lives here or if he just spends time here . . . keeping an eye on things.

"Why are you really here, Evan? You say you're protecting Zoey, but she doesn't even know you exist. And you and Lucinda—you're estranged. But she has to know you're here, she knows everything that goes on in this house. If you don't like each other, why does she let you stay?" I fire half a dozen questions at him, trying to throw him off a bit.

His jaw works, his eyes flicking toward a nearby darkened window before settling back on me.

"I already told you," he says finally. "It's complicated, you need to stay out of it, and don't ask questions."

"I would if I had that luxury. Nothing about this makes sense."

His expression hardens. "When Zoey was a baby, I saw things. Lucinda would leave her crying for hours. The things she said under her breath when she thought no one was listening—horrible, awful things I can't bring myself to repeat. Even now—she cuts her down, manipulates her, rewrites her reality right in front of her."

"And you know this . . . how?"

He slides a phone out of his pocket and pulls up a security app. Eight tiny squares fill the screen, each of them live broadcasting different parts of the house.

"If you always know what's going on . . . why are you here?" I ask, pretending it doesn't bother me that we've been under his eye all along. A chill runs through me, but I fight the shudder it wants to bring.

"I don't know." He sighs and puts his phone away. "Guess it gives me peace of mind."

I don't buy it for one second.

"And with my father getting sick this last year . . . I know Lucinda's behind it. She's the only one who'd stand to benefit from his death. She's made sure of that."

I let my eyes glisten with something that looks like sympathy.

Evan studies me like he's trying to gauge if I'm trustworthy or just another Lucinda.

If he only knew: I can be neither or I can be both.

I can be his best ally or his worst nightmare.

It all depends on him. Who he really is. What he's really doing here.

I lower my gaze, let my voice tremble on cue, and lie. "I don't doubt anything you're saying."

My mock validation mollifies his demeanor enough for me to confirm this is the path I need to take to get him to open up more. His shoulders drop. His brows unfurrow. He exhales long and deep.

"She did those things to me, too, when I was Zoey's age," I continue. "I'd hoped she'd changed by now . . ."

He shakes his head. "It's messed up. How can a mother do those things to her own kids?"

He drags his hand along his forehead, pressing his palm against his hairline and shoving his hair back.

"Your father seems like he adores her," I say.

"He doesn't know the real her. He's never seen it. She hides it. Always has," he says.

"How'd they meet anyway?"

"She was his secretary back in the day, when he ran a financial firm," he says. Quick math given Zoey's age and the timing of my departure tells me she had to have taken that job right around the time I left. "When my mother was still alive, the two of them had an affair. My mother mysteriously died six months into it. Any of that seem strange to you given what you know about Lucinda?"

I shake my head. "No. Not at all."

"My mother was a *saint*," he says, emphasizing that last word. "Then Lucinda came along, poured the charm on thick, figured out how to be his dream woman, and now here we are . . ."

"That's kind of her specialty. She used to do it all the time—only she usually snagged losers. Not men like your father."

"Once she got pregnant with Zoey, she started turning Dad against me, making things up, telling him I was harassing her . . ." He dumps his glass of bourbon into the kitchenette sink and pours a new one, sucking it down at room temperature in three gulps. "He cut me off, refused to talk to me, told me I was dead to him."

"God." I lift my fingertips to my lips. "I'm so sorry. She's an evil woman who's always destroyed anything in her path without a second thought. She gets off on controlling everyone around her. I told her earlier that I wanted to leave. She told me the kids and I are safer here. I don't think she's going to let us leave."

Evan pinches the bridge of his nose, clearly bothered by this information but not surprised.

"I . . . I need your help getting us out of here." I force a quiver into my voice. "Can you do that? Can you help us get out of here?"

I wrap my truth in vulnerability because there's nothing protective men love more than playing hero to a damsel in distress.

"Of course I can." He stands straighter, for once looking less defeated and more like a man on a mission. "You have my word."

It occurs to me on the way back to my room that if Evan has access to the security system and all the cameras Lucinda plastered around the property . . . she had to have been the one to give it to him.

Now all the holes in his story make sense. He's mixed enough fact with fiction to come off as quasi-believable . . . until now.

I can't trust Evan—but that won't stop me from using him.

24

The soaring walls here don't just creak—they carry. Words slip through them like water, muffled but distinct enough if you pay attention. Tonight I hear raised voices coming from one of the vents. There's no way to know what room they're being carried from, but it sounds like Evan and Lucinda. Their words are clipped, sharp, and low. I follow the sound, moving into the hallway, barefoot, silent, pressing my ear against the cool door to the apartment.

". . . what the hell are you doing?" Evan hisses. "We had an agreement. Now you're changing things without consulting me?"

I knew it.

Evan's nothing but Lucinda's lackey, here to help her do her dirty work.

I clamp a hand over my mouth to keep from gasping.

"Don't you dare lecture me." Lucinda's words crack like a whip. "She's mine and you know it."

I freeze, heart slowing, listening harder than ever.

"She's not your pawn," Evan growls. "You can do what you need to do and leave her out of it. It'll only make things more complicated and that's the last thing we need."

Are they referring to Zoey . . .

. . . or me?

Did Evan tell her I said she wouldn't let us leave? That I needed his help?

Footsteps grow closer to the door, too quick and light to be Evan's. I duck back into the bedroom, heart hammering in my ears. In the hallway, the apartment door creaks open, then clicks shut. Soon after, Lucinda's signature perfume wafts under our door, biting the air.

I wait until she's gone before peeking out and then knocking on Evan's door.

He answers in a fury, probably expecting her and not me. For a second, he looks like he might strike something—or someone. He folds when he realizes who it is.

"You lied to me," I say. It's risky, what I'm about to do. I know that. But anyone dumb enough to fall for Lucinda's tricks is dumb enough to fall for mine. "I thought I could trust you."

His jaw works, his chest rising and falling. Still, he says nothing.

"I can help keep Zoey safe," I add, shaping the words like an offering. This is what he wants. In fact, it's the only thing he wants. "If that's truly what you care about, we can help each other, but not if you're working for her. You told me not to trust her, now it seems like you're the one who can't be trusted."

"I told you it's comp—"

"Complicated," I finish his sentence. "I know. You've said that half a dozen times. I don't think it's as complicated so much as it's just a web of lies you're trying to keep straight."

He opens his mouth to say something, but I don't let him. I step closer, holding his gaze.

"Are you in love with her?" I ask. Under any other circumstances, the question would be ridiculous. But I can only think of one other reason he'd be this loyal to someone so diabolical. "Or is this about the inheritance?"

His mouth presses flat and his nostrils flare.

"Both?" I lift my brows.

He says nothing.

"You can plead the fifth all you want," I say, "but you'd be a fool to think you're anything more than a pawn in another one of her games. You're expendable. You mean nothing to her. She's using you the way she uses everyone. If she's led you to believe you're special, you're different, I promise you . . . you're not."

For a beat, the world is silent save for the pulse in my ears.

He nods once, slow, deliberate. "You don't think I know all of that?"

"Then why are you here? Why are you helping her?"

I keep my face dead serious and my thoughts sharper than that hunting knife tucked inside my bra.

"I really wish you would've taken my advice. You shouldn't have asked so many questions." He looks at me with pity in his eyes, his words landing like a death threat in disguise. And then he shuts the door in my face.

I'm getting us out of here.

Tonight.

And my only hope is a half-dying man who's maybe said a couple dozen words to me since we met.

25

The study smells wrong the second I cross the threshold—leather and dust and the sweet-fat tang of that lemon polish Lucinda worships, but braided through it is something sharper, a top note of chemical sweetness that doesn't belong to wood or paper or grief.

That's when I see him.

Rob.

Face down on the desk.

The angle of his neck is heavy, final. His cheek is pressed to the blotter, his fingers curled in an unnatural position, his wedding band a dull crescent under the lamp glow. A tumbler of spilled whiskey creates a river of amber across a stack of papers, the liquid fanning toward the edge like a slow golden tide. By the looks of how much liquor has soaked into the paper, he's been like this for a while.

"Rob," I say, my heart in the back of my throat.

He doesn't stir. Doesn't move. Doesn't breathe.

I reach for his forearm, giving it a good, hard shake to try and wake him on the off chance he's drunk and passed out.

But his skin is cool where the pulse should beat.

And his arm is stiff.

I'm calculating my next move when a scream tears loose behind me, unarranged, ugly, performative.

"Rob!" Lucinda appears in the study doorway, shoving me out of the way and throwing herself over her clearly dead husband. "God, no, no, no. Camille, call 9-1-1 . . . *now!*"

She wails.

She clutches at anything and everything.

She looks heavenward like light is a camera.

A modern Joan Crawford.

"Oh, God—somebody help!" I'm unsure who she's talking to—or who her intended audience is. Surely it isn't me? I can see through this like cellophane. And besides, she's always been an atheist. The only thing she's ever believed in is her ability to get whatever she wants. If there is a God, I pray he abandoned her the same way she abandoned him.

I grab the landline on the desk and dial 9-1-1.

"Hi, I have an unresponsive male," I tell the operator, my voice sanded and smooth. "Sixty-two? Sixty-three?" I pretend to not know his age, no reason to give Lucinda proof I've been digging. Using a nearby piece of mail, I rattle off their address. "No. There's no pulse," I answer her next question. The operator asks me to begin compressions. I look at Rob's neck, the way the tendons lie like broken strings, and judge the line between kindness and theater. "He's pretty cold," I answer. "There's stiffness. And I'm not sure I could get him on the floor."

He's easily eighty pounds heavier than me and rigor mortis is setting in.

The operator is quiet for a second before saying, "Units are on the way. Please stay on the line."

I set the receiver down carefully, mouth near the cradle so she can hear me breathe and we can both feel like I'm doing something.

"Help is coming," I tell Lucinda, and the words are so true and so pointless at the same time that it takes all the strength I have not to walk away right here, right now.

She's strangely calmer now. She's no longer touching him; she doesn't smear her grief across his skin in the form of fake tears. She simply kneels close enough that the closest security camera will catch this moment in real time.

I taste that wrong sweetness in the air again.

And I think of that small canister in the kitchen.

How Lucinda always measured from it with care and precision.

Thank God Zoey isn't here to witness this. She left for piano lessons a half hour ago, carpooling with a friend whose mom picked her up in a blacked-out Range Rover. Afterward, they're having a sleepover at her friend's house. I'm glad she isn't going to walk in on this—on her father's grayed mouth, on her mother's over-the-top performance, on the way a room turns colder by the second. I note the time on the clock and listen for a siren. It'll be four minutes, five at most in this zip code, the operator has informed me.

"Rob," Lucinda sobs at the floor by his feet. "Stay with me. Stay with me, darling. Don't leave me. I need you." Her hand hovers a half inch above his knee, then retracts like she touched a stove. Her mascara holds. Waterproof? Her lipstick hasn't smudged. Infallible? A single strand of auburn hair sticks to a tearstain at the corner of her mouth. Her full face of fresh makeup this time of night is . . . curious. But before I can think more of it, sirens sound in the distance.

I consider where I should be when uniforms start flooding the foyer. The problem with existing in a house you aren't supposed to exist in is that emergencies don't ask for your permission to expose you. Paramedics will want someone to answer questions while they perform their job. Then police will follow—police who are already on the lookout for someone matching my description. A body cam could catch me and this will all have been for nothing.

"You're going to have to wait for them at the door," I tell Lucinda. I expect her to argue but she doesn't. "They can't know I'm here."

She staggers to her feet like a woman who has never stood up in a rush in her life, but it's only because she wants them to see her first. The caring, doting wife needs to conduct this orchestra note by note. Perfume trails behind her, followed by sobs. The first thing she wants them to see will be her tears—tears that stopped a few minutes ago when she realized her performance was wasted on me.

I head upstairs to the bedroom, where I left the kids before the whole Evan confrontation. Georgiana was reading a Little Critter book to her brother. I told them I'd be right back, but it's been a while. I'm surprised they haven't come looking for me.

At the top of the stairs, I lurk in the shadows as the front door opens, listening to the cavalry of boots in the foyer. The jumble of voices. They come in a rush, two, three, a fourth behind them, equipment thudding, voices braided.

"Where is he?" a woman asks, calm yet commanding. I hear Lucinda direct them to the study. "When was the last time he responded? Any medical conditions we should know about?"

From up here, I listen as Lucinda cries, gasps, and lists symptoms irrelevant to the dead.

All the while, I stay unmoved and unnoticed, like I'm just another ghost who resides here.

As the Lucinda show continues and more emergency responders fill the house, I slide deeper into the hallway, seeking refuge behind the shadow of the grandfather clock where I am more part of the house than human.

I'm captivated by the entire scene until I hear footsteps that are *not* boots, followed by a hand tight on my shoulder.

Evan.

He's ashy, all color stripped from his face, his breath in short, violent pulls. For a heartbeat, he's the shape of a boy in a man's jacket.

"What happened?" he whispers, but I know he knows. His eyes flick past me to the foyer where the front door is open wide as a stretcher is brought in. His mouth opens and closes once before he decides not to speak.

"You know exactly what happened," I say under my breath.

Lucinda's wailing lurches into the hall in sharp shrieks. Below, a police officer is asking her questions while trying to soothe her at the same time. I listen to her shape a story she'll have well rehearsed and memorized by morning. For all I know, it's one she's been practicing for years.

Evan stands statue still, taking it all in from the shadows alongside me.

I wanted so badly to believe he was genuine, that he was just here to look out for his family, that he would be an ally, that he could help us escape Lucinda.

Now our only hope is dead.

"This wasn't the plan," he says. The sentence is ragged, shredded on the way out of him. "It wasn't supposed to . . ."

He doesn't finish his sentence.

I don't ask because I don't want to make more noise than we already have.

He presses the heel of his hand to his eye like pain could be rubbed out with friction, but something about it feels like a theater actor on stage. If Lucinda's trained him, she's trained him well.

"This is going to get bad." His vague and whispered words fade in and out as he tells me what I already know. "Real bad."

The pain in his voice is undeniable, but that doesn't make it believable.

He breathes once, long and endless like the breath might never end.

I'd give a penny for his thoughts if I had any extra pennies to give.

I almost feel sorry for him. He clearly had no idea what he was dealing with, at least not the extent of it. Now he's wrapped up in some murder plot with a woman who's a hundred times more cunning than he could ever be.

"She's going to pin this on you," I say.

Now that their plan has been executed, now that he's seen his dead father and the lengths Lucinda has gone to get her inheritance, I hope reality is hitting him hard upside the head. And maybe—just maybe—I can use that to my advantage so we can finally get out of here. Having a common enemy tends to bring people together.

In the doorway, the paramedics are doing the end tasks, hovering over a man who used to have a favorite joke and a favorite drink and a favorite way to fold socks, a man who has glasses, pajamas, and a closet full of clothes he'll never need to wear again.

Lucinda's weeping modulates to a manageable sob. She glances at her ring finger, twisting her wedding band back and forth, feigning anxiety and distress for her audience.

"Lucinda said something last time he was hospitalized, something about him wanting to change his will," I say softly, because I want to hear how the sentence sounds in a room with his bloodline in it.

"Really?" Evan asks. He jerks his head back, as if this is news to him. "What'd she say?"

"Just that Rob wanted to make sure she was taken care of."

"What would he have changed from before?" Evan ponders a question I can't answer for him.

In the foyer, a new policeman appears as if conjured by dread—blue button-down shirt, polite face, a notebook already open with a pen pressed against a clean page. Another one follows. The paramedic rattles off something I can't hear. I disappear a half step, returning back into the clock's shadow. Evan shifts so he's behind me.

Tonight we're ghosts together.

"I'm so sorry for your loss, Mrs. McClindon, but I do need to ask a few questions," the officer with the notebook says.

"Of course," she replies, already reorganizing her face into framed sorrow. "Anything you need. Do you—would you like some tea?" Her voice trembles prettily on *tea*. I imagine she'll use sugar from the *right* canister this time. If she's clever, she's already disposed of the small jar—and she is always clever.

I slide a glance to Evan. "I hope you look good in orange."

"She's going to get away with it," he whispers, eyes filled with fear and what I hope is remorse.

"People like her only get away with it because everyone else allows it," I say. "We won't. Not anymore. It ends now."

Lucinda steers the officer into the sitting room to answer his questions where the lighting is good and the furniture distractingly comfortable and luxurious. Another officer wanders the main floor halls with the intention of a man who knows he won't find anything. From what I can tell, they're treating this like a heart attack.

The paramedics talk in low voices that muffle together like background noise in a busy restaurant.

A radio crackles.

All of it drowns out Lucinda's answers to the officer's questions.

"Evan," I say, low, steady, "look at me."

He does as I instruct, only now it feels like a broken little boy is looking at me—not a man who'd spent years under the spell of the devil incarnate.

"I need you to hear me," I tell him. "Right now, no one knows I'm here. And no one should know you're here either. I'm going to hide in my room and you're going to hide in yours. If the police somehow find you, if you so much as breathe a word about me being here . . ." I let him finish my sentence in his head, hopefully imagining the worst. "If they ask who made the call, you say, *I don't know. I was upstairs. I came when I heard my stepmother scream.*"

His throat bobs.

"And you don't live here," I continue. "You were visiting. You heard the noise, you came down." My eyes flick toward the camera at the hall corner. "But you *don't* live here."

His hands flex once, everything about him crackling with an electric current I could stand under and get lit by. He flinches the way people do when a splinter comes out with the skin it lives in. Then he straightens. In the span of a couple of minutes, he somehow looks older and more dangerous, more *useful*. I can almost see his thoughts forming in real time, ruminating on the way Lucinda used him, finally accepting the fact that things always go according to her plans and he was nothing more than a means to an end.

"She's going to get everything," he says, and he means money but he also means she gets to control the narrative. "She'll spin this into a tragedy, come out looking like some poor widow, collecting sympathy and attention and tens of millions of dollars. And no one will suspect a thing because everyone loves her."

I shudder at the idea of people letting Lucinda into their homes, believing she's a "friend" and upstanding citizen, not knowing they're sharing their most intimate conversations and spaces with a literal child-abusing, murderous psychopath.

"She won't," I say. "Not if you can prove it was a crime she committed. Can you do that?"

He exhales a laugh that wants to be a sob and doesn't get permission. "Any dirt I have on her, she's got on me tenfold."

Stupid, stupid man.

There's not much I can do to help him now. And it pains me. Not because I feel bad for him, but because Lucinda doesn't deserve to win.

Over the course of the next hour, the first responders take their equipment away, the coroner comes to place Rob's body in a zipped bag, and the study changes from a place where a man died to an empty, beautiful room again.

When the front door is closed and the house returns to its silent status quo, Lucinda collects herself and heads toward the scene of the crime. The double doors are wide open, giving us an angled view inside from the top of the staircase. Evan and I watch in silence as she touches the back of his leather desk chair and looks at the spot where Rob's head was and lets her mask slip into one not intended for an audience.

"There's a small canister in the kitchen," I whisper to Evan. "I think she was using it to poison him. Do you know what I'm talking about?"

His eyes brim with validation as he meets mine. He nods.

"I think you should call in an anonymous tip. I'd do it myself, but . . ." I don't elaborate. I don't need to.

He nods as if he's accepting the assignment, but I'm pretty sure he's simply appeasing me. If he helped her—which I'm certain he did at this point—he'd only be accelerating the process of getting himself thrown away for second-degree murder. If anything, he'll destroy the evidence, though I'm positive Lucinda's one step ahead of him anyway.

"I need to get back to the kids." I leave him.

In our guest suite, Georgie and Jackson are a mess of Legos, books, giggles, and obliviousness as they jump on the bed like a makeshift trampoline. They're having so much fun, it takes them a minute to notice me.

"All right, bath time," I say as if it's the most exciting thing in the world.

Their giggles stop and they hop off the bed.

I truly have the best kids . . .

I don't know how I got so lucky, how such happy, healthy children came from someone who was raised by a predator.

But they're mine and I'll spend my dying breath keeping them safe.

While I clean the kids up for the night, my mind wanders all over the place. I think of the Reddit thread I fed last time and the woman who swore she saw me at a bus station two hundred miles away, and the way Will's eyes squinted with a hair of contempt when the reporter asked if he thought I left because I was in danger, the way the expression he gave was not for them, it was for me. I think of the shape outside my window and the gardener who looked like Will but wasn't. All of them tell me a fact I already know: Even if he's not here, his presence is.

Next I think of Evan realizing in real time that he was only ever a pawn. Then I think of Lucinda dosing out sweetness like toxic medicine—just another Venus flytrap, like my mother-in-law, Jacqueline. I think of Zoey whispering into her dying father's ear and the way she missed him so much she went into his study to get one of his favorite pens when he was in the hospital. And how Lucinda refused to let her visit him.

With Rob officially gone, the axis has shifted for every single person under this roof. Lucinda will inherit the estate and become disgustingly wealthy. The only man who truly loved Zoey is gone forever. And it's only a matter of time before Evan takes the fall for

Rob's death—assuming they run a toxicology report. They might not. But if they do, he's toast. And maybe he should be. He's not innocent in this. Just stupid. And being dumb isn't a crime—unless you're idiotic enough to kill someone.

My thoughts return to Zoey being at a sleepover, how it's her final night of being blissfully unaware that life as she's known it is about to change in ways she can't begin to imagine.

Will is still determined to find us and these tips are leading him closer than ever, which means I have to get the kids out of here—tonight if possible.

I run the numbers in my head, counting up what little money I have left.

It'd buy us a week, maybe two on the lam.

After that, we'll have nothing.

I try to convince myself there's a way out of this, but not before sleep takes a hold of me.

It's been an exhausting night.

I'll figure this out tomorrow.

26

Morning arrives like a bad hangover after a long night of unrefreshing sleep.

The house wears grief badly—too much lemon polish over the smell of last night, too many flowers clustered in vases that choke the air with sweetness. Word must travel fast in these circles because the floral arrangements haven't stopped arriving since eight AM.

Lucinda is a strangely beautiful ghost in a silk robe, eyes glassy, hair unbrushed yet perfectly messy, a tissue crushed in her fist like a prop.

The Reddit armchair detectives have stopped debating my whereabouts and have now switched to discussing Will's and my credibility and character. Familiar commentors argue in circles: *she's a monster, she's a saint, he's a devoted husband, he's a wolf in a suit . . .*

Lucinda has an appointment at nine with the funeral home, then another at ten with the pastor from the local Methodist congregation. I'm not sure when she found God, but she tells me this in a voice that keeps skipping like a scratched record, like she's practicing for the role of a lifetime: Robert McClindon's devastated widow.

To show her what a supportive, forgiving, and compassionate daughter I am, I make her some buttered toast—which she simply stares at—and then I pour her a coffee she doesn't drink.

She stands, sits, stands again.

More practice.

Zoey hasn't returned from her sleepover. I've yet to ask if she knows anything, but I'm assuming no.

While Lucinda pretends to grieve, I make the kids breakfast and focus on how to get us out of here. It'd be easy to throw our things in the car and bolt while she's off doing funeral things, but the fact of the matter is . . . I still need money—a detail that's further complicated by the fact that Lucinda's about to inherit millions.

If they do run toxicology on Rob and find something in his system, who's to say she won't spin a narrative that it was me? That I kidnapped my own children and came here asking for money? That I murdered Rob to punish her for saying no or because I thought I'd inherit something? Even if it makes no sense, Lucinda will find a way to make it make sense.

A dark SUV has been parked at the curb since seven this morning. It arrived shortly after one of the flower trucks—and never left. Its windows are so tinted, it's impossible to see through them; they just sit there reflecting the outside world, mysterious, anonymous.

Its presence is distracting.

I feel it even when I'm not looking, even when I'm deep in the belly of this expansive home, hidden away from the expansive front windows.

It could be anyone.

Will in a rental car.

A private investigator.

An agent from a three-letter agency.

Or someone investigating Rob's death? Though I'd think that'd be too soon . . .

While the kids eat, I head outside to take the trash out, locking the side gate on my way back in and moving the trash bin in front of it for camouflage. I push a patio chair slightly in front of the sliding glass door, not because it blocks anything—it doesn't—but because a small obstacle buys a half second and half seconds matter.

Afterward, I check the upstairs bedroom windows and wedge a makeshift dowel into the track of the one that never quite latches. I walk the kids through our code words again as though we're playing: "dragon" is "under the table," "thunder" is "in the bathroom and shut the door," "pancakes" is "don't move, don't make a sound."

An hour later, that SUV is still there, patiently idling.

I count the cash in my wallet. What I have will cover groceries and gas for a while if gas is cheap and we don't go too far and we sleep in the car and shower at truck stops. But after that, we're screwed.

I *have* to ask Lucinda for money.

But now is not the time. She's making calls about caskets and discussing music and muttering to herself about how many chairs they'll need and what kind of food to serve after the service.

I could ask Evan, but he's in a bad state right now. That and he doesn't exactly appear to be a man of means. He looks like someone who pawned his sleep for guilt years ago and has been living off the interest, barely making ends meet. If he *does* have money, he doesn't have access to it in a way that won't leave a trail.

There can be no trails once we leave.

I set the kids up in the family room with some cartoons, and Lucinda drifts back into the kitchen like a tide that keeps forgetting which direction it's supposed to go.

"The florist," she says. "They want a theme. A theme for death." She laughs like it's the most absurd thing she's ever heard, but at least she's not fake crying. "What color is grief, you think?" She has always loved questions that sound like philosophy but are actually about control. "Black? Black is cliché."

"Yellow means sorry," I say, and she flinches like I hit her. There's a darkness behind her eyes that disappears as fast as it showed up. She thinks I'm double-talking. "White," I correct myself. "Doves, lilies. Angels. White makes me think of hope and good things."

Her gaze relaxes. "White it is."

"Hey," I say while I have her attention. "There's been a dark SUV parked out front since seven o'clock. It's just been idling. Hasn't moved."

She frowns.

"Are you sure?" she asks. The belt of her robe hangs slack and her collarbone looks like it wants to cut through skin. She's always been thin, but lately she's practically vanishing.

"Yes." I keep my voice level, unsharpened. "I think we're being surveilled. Honestly, I'm worried it might be Will."

"I'd keep the kids inside today," she says, as if that's the only logical solution in this matter. She takes one sip of the coffee I poured her earlier and makes a face, setting the cup down as if it personally offended her.

Before she has a chance to comment on my idea, her phone rings. She answers immediately.

Funeral planning has a different voice than police questioning. It's softer, more padded, money wrapped around everything like a cashmere cardigan. I listen to her on the phone pretending she's listening to them, thanking them profusely for everything.

"Yes, Saturday. Yes, we want the chapel. No, the big one. We're expecting a large turnout." She paces the kitchen, stopping to smell a bouquet of Stargazer lilies. She plucks one from the bouquet and peels off its petals one by one, destroying its innocent beauty purely for her own entertainment.

Lucinda in a nutshell.

The front door opens and slams as soon as she gets off the phone. Within seconds, a glassy-eyed, red-faced Zoey is standing in the kitchen. Her overnight duffel bag lands at her feet with a heavy thump and she bursts into tears.

"When were you going to tell me about Dad?" Her voice is laced with anger, fury, and sadness. "I had to find out on Snapchat!"

Lucinda, for a moment, acts genuinely confused, but I remember Zoey saying Lucinda was very tech challenged. It makes sense she wouldn't understand how fast word travels among teenagers on social media. I imagine one parent found out, mentioned it to their kid, and the rest is history.

Lucinda's waterworks turn on like a spigot and she approaches Zoey with outstretched arms, forcing her into a hug she clearly doesn't want. Zoey bawls against our mother's shoulder, collapsing and letting Lucinda hold her.

It's a strange sight, like watching Satan himself offer comfort to a soul he's only ever tortured.

When it's over, Zoey wipes her tears on the backs of her hands, grabs her duffel bag, and runs upstairs before I can offer my condolences.

I peek out the sidelight windows by the front door. The SUV is still there. I snap a picture so I can ask Evan about it later. All this time, I've never asked him for his number. Then again, who'd have thought I'd ever need it?

For now, I think he sees me as an ally. We both have dirt on each other. We're both living here in hiding. I've technically kidnapped my kids and the whole country's trying to find me. He's an accomplice to second-degree murder. We might as well be pointing guns at each other in the form of owed favors.

I imagine him asking if I want him to make it leave, then I picture him stepping into the street with his intensity on his face and his gun in his pocket. He's not in the best state of mind at the moment, and the last thing I need is the kind of attention he might summon.

I need invisibility more than I need an empty curb.

By noon, the house has survived over twelve hours without Rob and decided it will continue to do so. Two men in gray suits arrive from the funeral home. Lucinda signs something with a trembling hand and then another thing with a steady one. After they leave, she stops in front of a hall mirror and does not fix her hair. She glances at the camera on a nearby shelf, pausing as if to wonder how that clip might look to someone on the outside.

I make the kids lunch and afterward, I think about Zoey.

"Stay here," I tell them. Someone should check on her and it's not going to be Lucinda. "I'll be right back."

I pad down to her room, listen for signs of life, then rap gently on the door three times.

"Go away," she says from the other side, voice muffled as if she's speaking into a pillow.

"It's just me," I say.

A few seconds later, the door opens. Zoey stands before me, eyes swollen, cheeks ruddy, nose rose red.

"I'm so sorry." I wrap her in a hug that I hope feels better than the one Lucinda gave her.

She melts against me, losing all composure.

"Will you lie down with me?" she asks when she comes up for air.

I eye the hallway, glancing toward the guest room door that I left closed. I don't want to leave the kids alone for too long . . . but Zoey's father just died.

I decide to leave her door open so I can hear any comings and goings while offering her some comfort at the same time.

On her queen-sized canopy bed, she curls up under plush blankets like she is still small. I lie beside her, not too close but not very far. She puts in her earbuds, stares at the ceiling, and does not press play on her phone.

Maybe she just wants to cancel the noise around her. The world is full of stimulation and distractions and sometimes it can be overwhelming.

She watches, unblinking, letting the world cave in on itself in heavy silence.

After a while, her eyes drift shut and her breathing steadies.

I slip out unnoticed and return to check on Jackson and Georgie.

"Mommy, can we go swimming today?" Jackson asks. "It's really sunny out."

I bite my lip. I wish I could take them swimming. I wish I could take them anywhere that's not . . . here. But that SUV is still outside and we're not yet in a position to leave Lucinda's.

Crouching down, I say, "So you know Grandpa Rob?"

They nod.

"He's been very sick, and last night he passed away," I say, injecting sadness in my voice. Most of the time I appreciate not being able to feel sadness, but in this case, I'm curious what it might feel like. Regardless, I have to model it for my children, so I do my best.

"What does 'passed away' mean?" Georgie asks. My children have never lost anything or anyone. Not a grandparent. Not a pet. Not even a stuffed animal. Maybe it's luck. Maybe it's also due to me sheltering them from every source of pain or negativity because no one ever did that for me.

"It means he went to sleep forever," I say in a way I hope they understand. "And Grandma Lucinda and Aunt Zoey are very, very sad. It would make them even sadder if they saw us having fun."

Georgiana's lower lip quivers, as if she somewhat understands.

Jackson pouts, but he doesn't argue. He's more upset about not being able to swim.

"It's going to have to be a quiet day. Puzzles and art and books," I tell them.

"When will they be done being sad?" my son asks.

"I don't know, honey." I cup his cheek and find myself distracted by his disheveled ponytail. He's looking quite boyish today. I should add a bow or a hair clip. If we have to leave—if we *get* to leave—his disguise has to be impeccable or it'll become distracting. A liability.

I set them up with crayons and coloring books for the time being, and when I stop to use the bathroom, I hear Evan on the other side of the wall, bustling around.

I knock once, softly.

"Yeah?" His voice through the drywall is thin but it's there.

"Can you meet me in the hall?" I ask.

"Yes."

I tell the kids to stay put, and I head to the apartment door.

"There's been an SUV parked outside all morning. Hasn't left," I tell him. "Tinted windows. Just sits there idling. Do you know anything about it?"

"I saw." Worry lines spread across his forehead like deep fissures. "You think they're investigating Lucinda?"

I want to slap Evan and shake him at the same time.

"No," I say. "It's too soon for any of that. I think it might be my husband . . . or an investigator. Someone knows we're in the area."

Evan's eyes spring to life when he remembers there are *other* possibilities. I don't blame him. I bet he hasn't slept a wink since last night and all he's been thinking about is the life sentence he may or may not receive when the smoke clears after the funeral.

"I hate to ask, but I need money," I say. "Not much. Just . . . something to get us by for a bit."

He doesn't answer for a full five heartbeats.

"I don't have a lot." He drags a hand along his unshaven jaw.

"I know," I say. "I don't have a lot either. But at least you have a place to stay and you're not being stalked by someone who wants to take your kids away and send you off in handcuffs. You have options, Evan. We don't."

"Is there anything you can sell?" he asks.

My jaw wants to hit the floor. He's really not going to help us? After everything? I thought we were on the same team, which was anti-Lucinda. If he doesn't help me get out of here, in a way, he's helping her even more.

"I don't," I say. "I sold everything I had to get here. Do you?"

He chews the inside of his lip. "I might have a few things."

I lift my brows, waiting for him to elaborate.

"It'll take me a few days, but I'll see what I can scrounge up," he finally says.

A few days is more time than I have, but leaving without money isn't an option.

"Thank you." I wrap my arms around him for positive reinforcement, to make him feel like a hero. "I couldn't do any of this without you."

We go our separate ways, and while I've never been one to panic, today I almost feel the need to breathe into a paper bag.

By dinnertime, Lucinda wanders the halls with a pen, circling items on a list for the post-funeral reception and then crossing them out and then circling them again. Her vigor makes it seem like she's planning a bridal shower, not a burial.

She stops in front of me and says, "I need your help."

An old muscle in my jaw tenses at the phrase.

"Could you go into Rob's closet and find me his navy YSL suit? And the paisley tie that has hints of burnt orange in it? It was always his favorite. Chicago Bears colors but classy, you know? He should look like himself."

"Of course." I find my way to a closet that smells like cedar and success and locate the suit and tie. I also grab a pair of cognac leather loafers he'll never walk in again. When I bring the items to her, she touches the jacket sleeve like she's petting a beloved animal.

"I still can't believe it," she says, the lie at home on her tongue.

She leans against the wall and slides down to the floor, graceless for once.

"I'm so tired," she whispers. I crouch and level with her.

The camera watches us from its corner like an all-seeing eye.

I angle my back to it.

"You need to sleep," I tell her. It's ironic, nurturing her when she never once did that for me. "Eat—then sleep."

She closes her eyes as if that order is too tall, and I promise to bring soup and put it on a tray. We'll both pretend it's love.

Maybe with some rest and a few calories, she'll be in a place to finish the conversation I tried to have earlier about leaving.

I get her situated before making dinner for the kids and Zoey. Boxed macaroni and cheese. Microwaved chicken nuggets. Sliced bananas. Zoey doesn't eat, but she seems to appreciate not having to be alone.

Outside, the SUV remains. Still unmoved. The sky transitions to a darker blue. A neighbor walks a poodle-mix dog that looks like a man in a dog costume—serious, bearded, resigned. Creepy humanlike eyes. The expensive mutt pees on the same shrub twice. The neighbor doesn't so much as glance at the SUV because people in nice neighborhoods have the luxury of being able to mind their own business and walk their dogs without worry.

Inside, the house groans and cameras watch.

I make one last slow lap of the downstairs, my folded knife pressed against my ribs like a trusty sidekick.

Will used to talk about inevitability the way other men talk about weather.

"Some things we just can't fight," he'd say as if he were saying something profound. "Some things are beyond our control and all we can do is deal with them when we're forced to."

If he's not in that car, he's in another.

If he doesn't arrive today, he will tomorrow.

He has the whole country believing he's generous and grieving, righteous and virtuous. A good dad. God, the world loves a good dad. People act like there aren't enough of them anymore, but the truth is the good ones don't make headlines the way the bad ones do.

Either way, I know he's close.

I feel it.

Before bed, I adjust our blinds so they're open, but I close the curtains and untie the cord. Once the kids are asleep, I turn off the lamp so I can look out the window, see and not be seen. In that dark moment, my reflection is pale and unfamiliar, a woman with short brassy hair and tired, wild-animal eyes.

Evan said he'd scrounge money up for me in the next few days. Rob's funeral is in three days, which will keep Lucinda and Zoey occupied and out of the house.

If everything lines up the way I think it will, that's our chance to leave.

I sleep easier tonight knowing we have a plan, an out, an escape from Lucinda, from Will, and from living in hiding with a house full of strangers.

27

The house is a mausoleum the second day after Rob's death—heavy with the kind of grief that's manufactured to look perfect from the outside.

Lucinda and Zoey have been at the funeral home since this afternoon, making decisions about flowers and caskets, music and photo displays—the kind of details Lucinda thrives on, details that make her grief appear genuine.

Their absence leaves the house empty in a way I wasn't expecting, a way that doesn't make me feel safe, but rather exposed, like they were almost serving as human shields. I've probably double- and triple-checked every lock on every door and window in this house at least half a dozen times since they left.

I'm cleaning up the kitchen after dinner, the kids occupied with cartoons in the family room, when a dark shadow outside catches the corner of my eye.

I choke on my breath and drop the glass I was washing in the sink.

It shatters into a million pieces.

"Damn it . . ." I mutter when I realize it's Evan. He's standing on the back patio, motioning for me to step out and join him.

"We have to save her," he says before I can slide the door all the way shut. The scent of unwashed hair wafts off him, carried by the summer breeze of this strange, sunny day. He looks and smells like he hasn't showered in a minute, but this is nothing new.

I glance up, poker-faced. "Save whom?"

"Zoey." He steps closer, the tension in him wound tight, his hands clenched into balls at his sides. "Lucinda has never loved her. Not once. And now, with Rob gone . . ." He shakes his head, jaw clenched. "Lucinda's going to neglect her worse than before. You know what that does to a teenager? To someone already fragile? Lucinda's going to ruin her entire life before it even begins."

He's not wrong.

But I'm not sure how he thinks either of us are in any position to "save" her. We don't have money and Lucinda's not going to just let Zoey leave.

He probably hasn't slept in days and he's not thinking clearly.

I keep my expression soft, measured, though inside I'm already cataloging the use of his word "fragile." "So how do you think we can protect her, exactly?"

His eyes flick to mine, searching, as if I might hand him a blueprint. Then he paces, deep in thought, like the weight of Zoey's future is so heavy he can't set it down, so he just carries it.

"Take her with you," he says like he's having some kind of eureka moment. "When you leave in two days, take her with you. I'm working on getting you some money. I'll make sure you have enough."

"Evan." I press my lips flat, trying my best to disguise my true feelings on his idiotic idea. "I'm not kidnapping Zoey."

His breathing turns harder. He won't look at me.

I place a hand on his shoulder. "Look. I'd love nothing more than to save her from a life with Lucinda. But I can't. I don't have the means or resources. I've got two small children I'm trying to keep safe. My hands are tied. A husband and apparently an entire country are looking for me. You know that."

His pale eyes make their way to mine and he nods like he understands, but there's no air of acceptance about it.

"So you've sold some stuff?" I ask, keeping the conversation on track.

"I've lined up a buyer for a couple things." The ambiguity of his answer doesn't make me feel any better.

"How much do you think you can get?"

His mouth bunches at one side. "Hoping three, maybe four hundred."

It's a fraction of what we need.

I hide my disappointment in the form of gratitude. "That would be amazing, Evan. Thank you. If you could come up with any more . . . I'll pay it all back with interest, once I get on my feet. I promise."

He drags in a jagged lungful of damp night air.

"They're probably going to be back any minute," I say. "They can't see us together."

"How can I keep her safe?" His eyes water and his voice breaks. This man isn't dangerous. Not in the way I first thought. The only dangerous thing about him is that he has no control over his emotions. "If the police find out about Rob . . . I'm the one going down. Zoey'll be on her own."

The question hangs between us. He looks like he's about to say something else, his mouth parting, his hands unclenching, some truth bomb about to slip out—when the world snaps.

The lights inside die, the AC units cut off mid-hum, and the house folds into darkness so thick it's suffocating.

The sound of shattering glass follows—sharp, violent, unmistakable.

Evan's eyes go wide. Mine narrow.

Because whatever was coming has arrived.

28

The glass is still crunching somewhere in the house when instinct takes the wheel.

I have Georgie and Jackson by the hand and sleeve respectively, dragging them upstairs and telling them to be quiet as a mouse.

"Thunder. Remember our code words?" I whisper, keeping my voice light. But the way they look at me tells me they know this isn't a game. Their wide eyes search for permission to be afraid. I give them none. I press my finger to my lips and whisper the rules, "No sounds, no matter what."

Once we're upstairs, I repeat, "Thunder."

As practiced, they hide in the bathroom, tucking their tiny bodies underneath the vanity.

I tell them I'm going to lock the bedroom door behind me and they're not to come out for any reason until they hear my voice.

My heart hammers with a force so violent it hurts. I turn, spine pressed to the wall, ears straining, hand clasped at my bra where I can feel the smooth metal of the hunting knife handle. I dig it out and press it into my palm before heading to the pitch-black hallway.

Evan bolted when we heard the glass. I imagine he's hiding in his apartment, but I hope I'm wrong. I hope he went to get his gun and he'll be back any minute.

But each minute that passes feels longer than the one before, the house growing more silent with each tempered breath.

I'm not sure how much time has passed when the narrow beam of a flashlight sweeps across the top of the staircase—followed by heavy footsteps that don't belong to a rail-thin fifty-year-old woman or a teenage girl. The white beam motions left, then right, catching frames, doorways, and floorboards before it lands square in my face, blinding my vision.

I duck down behind a half-moon console table and freeze against the wall, but it's too late.

I squint out from behind the furniture piece, desperate to see, but all I can make out is a tall figure with broad shoulders. A familiar build I know too well.

He steps closer and the beam lowers just enough to keep his face obscured, but I don't have to see it to know who it is.

He found us.

My breath stops on its own, my lungs screaming for air but unable to make a sound. He closes the distance, drops the flashlight, grabs my shirt collar to raise me up, and pins me to the wall with the weight of a man who never truly loved me—he only loved owning me.

The knife that was in my hand a moment ago is long gone, lost in the shuffle, vanished into the dark.

His hand digs into my shoulder, his fist gripped around my neck as he brings his lips to my ear. I brace myself, waiting for the threat he's been saving for weeks, the message he's been dying to personally deliver.

I lift my chin just enough to keep his hand from closing on my throat.

Then I remember the heavy vase on the console, the one made of thick cut crystal. My hands scramble for it, my fingertips grazing the edge of the table. It's just out of reach, but I fight like hell.

The already black world around me turns a shade darker as his hand presses harder on my larynx.

Somehow, through the struggle, I manage to get us closer to the vase. Hooking my fingertips on its lip, I grab it, slide it nearer, fasten my grip, and swing it as hard as I can at his head.

It shatters against his temple, making a cracking sound like a bone splitting.

He staggers back, blood sluicing down his forehead, shining in the fading light of the flickering flashlight on the ground.

"You're going to pay for this. For what you did to me. To this family." The low, gravelly voice threatening me . . . doesn't belong to Will.

My heart pounds but I stay frozen.

Who *is* this?

Is this the person who was camping out in that SUV? Some keyboard warrior or armchair detective? Because it isn't Will. And a PI or federal agent wouldn't break and enter and attempt to choke someone to death.

I drop to the ground, fishing for the flashlight with shaking hands.

Before I can reach it, he kicks it away.

It skids down the hall, coming to a stop in the wrong direction, leaving us both in the dark.

This game? It's officially anyone's.

I'm cornered, literally. My back is pressed against the door to the apartment. Surely Evan heard this commotion?

Where the hell is he?!

The mystery man closes in on me again, slow and deliberate, purposely intimidating. His hand brushes my cheek, mockingly gentle. "Look at you. I could squeeze the life out of you in five seconds flat, and I have every reason to. But you're not even shaking. That's . . . not going to be very fun for me."

"The kids aren't here," I lie. "If that's what you want."

His grip slams me harder against the wall. My ribs ache. He's too strong. I can't match this kind of physical force.

"You'll never find them," I lie again. "No one will. I've made sure of that."

He leans closer, lips curling, breath hot against my skin.

Whoever this is wants to scare me.

I won't give him that.

If this were Will, I'd be rattling off a million barbs meant to dig deep into the flesh of his fragile ego. I'd tell him I never loved *him*, only what he gave me—a comfortable life, nice things, a place to hide. Two children I'd die to protect.

The intruder's hand presses harder against my throat. If it was Will, I'd keep speaking, every word designed to slice deeper than the one before it. I'd tell him he's diabolical. That the kids are going to spend the rest of their lives knowing their father murdered their mother, who kept them hidden because of how dangerous he was. I'd tell him that when the truth comes out, it'll contradict the story he's been feeding the media and he'd be a laughingstock.

It would send him into a rage and rages make people sloppy.

But this isn't Will.

I have no idea what this man wants . . . other than to kill me.

Zoey and Lucinda should be home any minute—unless, of course, their absence was no coincidence. And where the hell is Evan hiding? He heard someone break in, he has a gun, and he just left me? All that talk about protecting people, all the times he flashed his gun, it was to make up for the fact that he was nothing but a coward.

It's almost as if someone cleared the stage for this man's entrance . . .

"You stupid, *stupid* woman," the man spits his words into my face. His breath tastes like stale coffee and hatred, and he speaks like someone trying to disguise their voice. Something about the tone is familiar and unnatural, though I can't quite place it. "I don't give a shit about your fucking kids."

My world tilts.

I open my mouth to respond, to stall, to fight with words since my body is failing me—and then a gunshot rips the air open.

The flash of the shot lights the dark hallway enough for me to see the face of the man who attacked me before his body collapses at my feet like dead weight. I'm frozen. Unable to breathe. Unwilling to believe my own eyes but knowing I don't have a choice.

The gunshot still echoes in my ears and the tang of gun smoke fills the hallway air. My pulse rams against my chest painfully hard, like it's trying to escape. In a way, I've already left my body. I'm observing from afar, watching a movie scene play out.

I stare at Evan's dark, lifeless body on the floor . . . and realize I'm not free.

Not yet.

Because the only question louder than the ringing in my ears is: Who pulled the trigger?

29

Evan lies in a heap at my feet, his blood seeping into the hardwood as if the house itself wants to drink him. His hand is curled in the shape of my neck, his jaw slack, his eyes fixed on a wall he'll never see again. My chest heaves but not from panic—from confusion.

My ears are still ringing with the gunshot when I see the slight figure in the distance.

Zoey.

She stands several feet down the hall, a handgun steady in her small hands. She's not trembling. And this is not the uncertain posture of a child who stumbled into a nightmare. Her stance is practiced, collected, poised.

She lowers the weapon with care and smiles at me. Slow. Sly. Knowing.

In that moment, all I see is Lucinda.

But I remind myself Zoey just saved my life.

"I never liked him anyway." Her voice is calm, almost bored. "He was always so obnoxious. Way too confident in his ability to manipulate people. Kind of like your husband, Will." She steps closer, nudging Evan's arm with her foot like he's trash to be moved aside. "I saw through your husband from the very first interview."

Interview.

Her words land sharp.

This means she's been following the case.

Watching the coverage.

Listening to podcasts.

Probably reading the Reddit threads.

Probably *participating* in the Reddit threads.

Was it Zoey all along? Was she the one giving away our location?

The sight of her—the gun now hanging casually at her side, the smirk that belongs to a predator who hasn't yet decided on mercy—presses at my spine like ice. She's a teenager, yes, but teenagers are nothing if not unpredictable. And this one has been polished by Lucinda's equally unpredictable hands. There are moments I see myself in her—and then there are moments like this. She is everything I never wanted to be, and ironically everything I should've been at her age.

Ruthless, careful, always one step ahead.

She tilts her head, her hair falling into her eyes. "Where are the kids?"

The way she asks—flat, pointed, knowing—sends another chill through me.

I don't want to tell her . . .

And I can't.

Because Zoey might be the most dangerous one of all.

30

The silence after the gunshot is a vacuum, the kind that pulls truth into its center whether you're ready to hear it or not. Evan's dark cherry blood inches toward the baseboards like it wants to seep into the foundation.

Zoey lingers, planted in the hallway with the gun dangling casually at her side, her eyes gleaming with something that doesn't belong to a girl her age.

I listen for the sound of small footsteps, hoping against hope that my kids don't come out to investigate. They've had to have heard everything. I'm sure they're terrified.

"Wait," I manage, my voice slow, careful, though inside my nerves are screaming. "You knew who Evan was?"

She rolls her eyes, the gesture pure teenage contempt. "Of course I know who Evan is. He's my dad. My *real* dad. I'm not even a McClindon."

The words should land heavy, yet Zoey appears unaffected.

"Wait," I say as I try and wrap my head around this. "I thought he was Rob's son?"

She smirks. "Yeah, right. Rob never had any kids. He was just some random rich guy Mom hooked up with back in the day. When she realized she was already pregnant by Evan, she told Dad it was his because duh, who'd you rather have help you raise a kid? Someone with money or . . . a lowlife idiot?"

"I'm confused."

"About what? It's pretty simple."

"Why was he living here?" I ask. "Why did he want me to think he was Rob's son?"

"Because he was crazy? I don't know. You saw him. The guy looks like he's got a screw loose or something." She huffs. "It sucks he's my real dad."

It makes sense now why he was so worried about keeping Zoey safe. She wasn't his half sister, she was his *daughter*. And of course he didn't care if Rob died—Rob meant nothing to him. The sooner he died, the sooner Evan would get his payout. It was never about loyalty to Lucinda.

He wasn't lying when he said this was complicated.

"Yeah, but why did Lucinda stay in touch with him?" I ask. "Why'd she even tell him the baby was his?"

Zoey shrugs. "I think she thought she could convince him to kill my dad so she could take all his money . . . but Evan saw through it, turned the tables, and blackmailed her. Threatened to tell Dad the truth about me and about her plans unless she paid him off. But she couldn't pay him off because she never actually had access to any bank accounts. All she had was a credit card with a monthly spending limit. She knew if Evan told Dad the truth, he'd leave her and she'd be back to having nothing. No mansion. No Mercedes. No country club."

"Okay, so I get why Evan blackmailed her, but why'd she let him live here?"

"Why does she do anything?" Zoey counters. "Because it benefits her in some way. I think her whole plan was to make him take the fall for the murder. And now that he's dead? Easy."

"But you killed him," I remind her. "You're not worried she's going to make you take the fall for that? Everyone's expendable. Everyone's a pawn. You think she'll protect you?"

"I might be young." Zoey appears unfazed. "But I'm not stupid."

She says this with such frightening conviction that I believe her.

A question dances on the tip of my tongue—I want to know how much of this Zoey orchestrated, but if she hasn't been honest with me yet, why would she start now?

"No more lies, no more secrets," I say, quickly adding, "We're sisters."

I'm hopeful mentioning the sister thing will forge a bond we don't quite have yet, but if she's anything like me, manipulation doesn't work on her.

"Camille—*Gabrielle*," she says, a sly smile on her tilted face. "Do you not remember one of the first things I ever said to you? *Everyone lies here.* It's how you survive with her. You of all people should know that."

For a moment, I don't know if I'm staring at a child or a miniature Lucinda. A girl who can pull a trigger without remorse, smile through the splatter, and lay out an indictment like a seasoned prosecutor three times her age.

I straighten my spine. "How am I supposed to trust you now?"

She lifts a shoulder as if it's not her problem. "Can you really trust anyone these days?"

I know the answer to that question all too well. I was simply hoping to guilt her, but every time she opens her mouth, I realize what I'm dealing with.

Someone who can't feel guilt, remorse, or love.

Someone created by Lucinda.

Someone like *me*, but less restrained.

Like a baby scorpion, too young to control its venom.

"Why did Evan want to kill me?" I fold my arms. Maybe she'll be honest. Maybe she won't. But I have to ask.

"Because he's a nutjob."

"That's not a reason to kill someone."

She chuffs. "Something about him being worried you were going to take some of the inheritance Lucinda promised him. Since Rob left everything to her and you're her biological daughter, I think he was worried you were going to mess everything up for him."

It's plausible. Especially since he was clearly unstable, obsessive, and cryptic. Every interaction with him left me questioning whether he was for or against Lucinda, and he really had me believing he cared about Zoey's well-being. In the end, he was just a dumber, less competent Lucinda.

"Who broke the glass?" I ask next. "I was with Evan when it happened, then he ran off."

"You're a smart woman. Who do you think?"

The entire thing seemed carefully orchestrated . . . Evan being with me while an "intruder" broke in, Evan disappearing, a man choking me in the dark, Zoey and Lucinda returning just in time for Zoey to shoot Evan in the back. Knowing Lucinda, she planned everything down to the last detail, probably convinced Evan to kill me for whatever reason, then staged the break-in and sent Zoey to handle the rest.

A hundred more questions swarm my thoughts, but all of them are overridden with one because despite all the chaos, the house is eerily quiet and Lucinda is mysteriously absent.

"Where are my kids?" I ask.

"Probably wherever you left them? I don't know."

I scramble to my feet, sprint into the bedroom, and shove myself through the bedroom door—a door that should've been harder to open because I locked it behind me. I know I did. I triple-checked.

The bathroom is empty and nothing's out of place—except one thing.

Along the wall, where a framed art piece had been mounted this entire time, is a small square door on hinges, the opening just wide enough for children . . . or a small adult.

I peek my head inside, determining it's an old laundry chute.

Laundry chutes usually lead straight down to a basement.

"Zoey!" I turn around to find her two feet behind me. It gives me a startle. "Did you know this was in here?"

"The laundry chute? Yeah. All the bathrooms have them. It's an old house."

"Where does this go? Can someone access this room from inside the chute?" I know the second question sounds crazy, but I'd have seen my children leave the bedroom had they left it, and I know they wouldn't have magically found the chute on their own.

Zoey rolls her eyes, annoyed at my questions. "Who knows with this creepy place."

"Where's Lucinda?" I spit out my next question with heart-stopping urgency. I'd ask how Lucinda knew where my kids were hiding, but I'm not in the mood to be met with more teenage attitude. I simply need to find my children.

"Why are you so angry with me? I just saved your life"—her brows knit—*"sister."*

She steps closer, her sneakers smearing Evan's blood across the tile in a careless streak.

"Just . . . help me find my kids." I let my now-useless mask fall. "Please. Where's your mom?" I ask again, this time referencing Lucinda as *her* mom.

She sure as hell isn't mine. Never was. Never will be.

Zoey shifts her weight, wiping her bloody shoe on a bathroom rug, unconcerned with the gore she's leaving behind. "Couldn't tell you."

"You have to."

"I can't," she says, angrily insistent. "I literally don't know."

This is bad.

"I need you to help me," I say. "Find Lucinda. Find my kids. Just . . . help me. *Please.*"

Zoey cocks her head. "I just saved your life. Now you're bossing me around like I'm your personal assistant."

I take a step closer, lowering my voice into something intimate, confessional, yet dominant. "I'm bossing you around because I need your help. Because we're sisters. And because whatever you are, I'm the same. We can be an unstoppable force—or each other's worst enemies. Your choice."

A spark of something comes to life in her eyes.

And we disappear into the recesses of this ancient house to find my children.

31

Terror has a taste, metallic and sharp, and it floods my mouth as I'm standing in a musty cinder block basement with low ceilings and cobwebs at every turn. The open hole above me lines up perfectly with the laundry chute in my bathroom, but my children are nowhere to be seen.

I search every corner, yelling their names in vain.

Their AirTags only tell me they're in the house—wherever they are, I can only pray they're still alive.

I sprint upstairs, my hand slapping doorframes as I round corners and my bare feet skidding across polished floors. My breath is ragged and shallow.

Then I hear it—the wail of sirens in the distance followed by flashes of red and blue that grow brighter and closer by the second.

A neighbor must've heard the shot.

Gunshots always summon the law.

I'm almost to the foyer when I spot Zoey heading to the door. She strolls with terrifying calm, as if she's been waiting for this exact cue. She must feel me behind her because before her hand so much as touches the knob, she turns to look at me.

"If you repeat anything I told you earlier," she says with ice and a threatening smile, "just know I'm telling them who you are."

The instant she lets the cop in, she begins to sob—a page straight out of Lucinda's book, her shoulders folded over, her knees pretending to give out. She braces herself against the responding officer who catches her fall and attempts to hide his confusion.

"He's . . . he's upstairs," she wails. "I shot him. The man who broke in . . ."

The cop mumbles something into his radio, then turns back to her. "Are you alone?"

Zoey turns, lifting a shaking finger pointed toward the shadows where I'm standing.

"No," she says, sniffing. I hold my breath, waiting to hear how she identifies me. "We have company in town. My mom and I came home . . . I saw the broken glass in the back . . . I heard something upstairs . . ."

She stops to sob a bit more, dramatic effect I suppose.

I exhale. She hasn't said my name . . . yet.

"The man was trying to hurt her," she continues, wiping fake tears on the backs of her blood-stained hands. "He threw her against the wall, he was threatening her, he had his hands around her throat . . ."

"Are you all right, ma'am?" the cop asks me.

I nod just before Zoey runs into my arms and buries her face against my chest.

Two more officers walk in, armed with flashlights, their hands on their holsters just in case.

"He's upstairs," I tell them. "In the hallway on the right."

"We still need to find my kids," I whisper to her.

"Mommy!" The sound of Georgiana's voice has never sounded so sweet. Within seconds, two pairs of little arms are wrapped around my hips. "We heard a loud noise in the hall! Then we heard Grandma Lucinda talking to us through this hole in the wall, behind a picture. She told us to jump down like a slide. We landed in a laundry basket. Then she took us into this room behind a door that looked like a bookcase. She said we had to stay with her until it was safe to come out."

"It was really fun!" Jackson adds.

I stop. Replay my daughter's words.

Lucinda kept my children *safe*?

To my left, Lucinda steps forward, a smug, satisfied look on her face. I want to ask why, but the answer doesn't matter. Not after all the lies. Not after all the killing. Not after all the chaos she's coordinated.

"We're leaving," I tell her.

"I wouldn't advise that," Lucinda speaks like the voice of reason she is not and has never been. Upstairs I hear one of the officers say they've recovered the weapon. "The police are going to want to bring you in for questioning. You think it's wise to leave now?"

Leaving could incriminate me if my identity gets out—something Lucinda wouldn't hesitate to do if I go against her wishes.

My children look at me, wide eyed, bewildered, exhilarated almost. They watch my face as if they're looking for guidance of some kind, so I snap back into the role they need me to play.

I gather them close. "It's okay. Everything's fine. There was a bad guy in the area, but we're all safe now."

I want to lecture them about disobeying my orders. I've told them time and again to stay put, and when they hid, I told them not to come out for anyone but me.

But now is not the time.

Instead, I kiss their foreheads and nonchalantly make sure the AirTags on their wrists are still snug.

I give them grace because I imagine they were scared and the only thing they know about Lucinda is she's their grandma who bakes cookies, lets them swim in her pool, and fawns over their adorableness. Of course they trust her.

The only question that remains for now . . . is how did she know where to find them?

32

I'm huddled in the foyer with the kids and officers, trying to piece together how Lucinda so easily accessed my children. Why was the laundry chute hidden with a picture? Was it intentional or was it simply an eyesore conveniently covered? Knowing Lucinda, it had to be the former.

"Mrs. McClindon, I'm so sorry you're dealing with this after everything else you've gone through," one of the officers tells her.

I recognize him from the night Rob died.

Two dead bodies in the McClindon house in one week—wouldn't that set off some alarm bells?

She nods, mouthing a silent "Thank you" as she dabs an invisible tear at the corner of her eye. "It's unfortunate. I spent all day at the funeral home only to come home to an intruder? I'd heard rumors of break-ins in the neighborhood, but I never thought . . ."

Lucinda lets her voice trail into nothing because telling the truth isn't an option.

"I was in the garage," Lucinda says, her voice threaded with tremor, soft but controlled. "On the phone with my sister-in-law. My daughter went inside while I finished my call, then I came in to find the power had been cut. Next thing I know, there's a man's voice . . . and a gunshot . . . the first thing I thought about was my daughter—and our family friend staying with us, but after I heard their voices I knew they were okay. Thank God."

The cop turns to Zoey. "What about you? What did you see? What did you hear?"

She brushes up against her mother, resting her head on Lucinda's shoulder for mock comfort. "Like my mom said, we got home. She was on the phone in the car. I came inside and noticed the power was out. I was headed to my room to grab my flashlight when I heard glass break. I got scared and hid for a little bit, then I heard something loud in the hall. A man's voice. Then hers." She points to me. "I came out and he was shoving her around, threatening her. He wouldn't stop. He was so much bigger than her. I didn't know what to do. I saw a gun on the floor. . . . it must've been his? I . . . I just picked it up and aimed it at his back and pulled the trigger. I've never shot a gun before. I didn't even think it would go off. It really scared me when it did . . ."

My stomach twists at how Oscar-worthy Zoey's performance is.

The tears.

The tremble in her voice.

The eyes darting everywhere.

It hits me now that she's telling the story with as much detail as she can . . . for me.

Not to mention, she's intentionally not mentioning my name or that we're sisters.

It's unexpectedly protective.

Between the three of us, if we stick to the same story, suspicion will stay off Lucinda, my identity will remain a nonissue, and no judge in their right mind is going to charge a thirteen-year-old with murder done in self-defense.

The power flickers on. A minute later, one of the officers returns to inform us someone had flipped off the main breaker in the garage.

"Mrs. McClindon, I'm really sorry to ask this, I know it's been a difficult week for your family, but given what happened tonight, we are going to need statements from the three of you," the main officer says. "Would you all mind coming down to the station for a bit?"

Lucinda doesn't flinch at the suggestion, but she does yawn.

Anything for sympathy.

"I'm quite exhausted," she says, "but I'd never want to keep you from doing your job. I'm just not sure how much help I can be other than what I've already shared, but I'll try my best. I'm just glad my daughter and our guests are safe," she says to him while she's looking at me.

"We appreciate that. Happy to drive you guys there and back if need be," a second officer offers.

"That won't be necessary," I interject. "We'll drive ourselves."

This could be my only chance to leave with the kids if my real name somehow gets out between now and then. Now that these officers have all seen me and I'm the key witness in Zoey's self-defense claim, it's only a matter of time before someone realizes I fit the description of the missing Arizona woman who "kidnapped" her children.

"We'll be right behind you," Lucinda says, but before they leave, she adds, "My friend's daughter is visiting with her kids. She's going through a divorce at the moment and now this happens? Poor thing. Before we go, I need your word that you won't make this more traumatic for her than it's already been."

At face value, it would appear she's crafting a narrative before they have a chance to piece one together themselves. This coupled with the fact that she kept my children safe from Evan . . .

What is she doing?

What's her ulterior motive? Because she always has one.

Lucinda lowers her lashes, wearing grief and exhaustion like a shimmering veil.

"My late husband was *very* good friends with Chief Whitlock," she adds softly. "Rob always said how grateful he was for how safe you kept this community. I'm just glad he wasn't here to see this happen in his own home. I know he would've tried to protect us, and I shudder to think about how that would've gone."

The officer's eyes shift with recognition. Rob was a prominent man. McClindon is a respected name. I watch his sympathy deepen in real time as the entire room bends toward her.

"Whenever things are hard, I like to remind myself they can always be worse," she says for dramatic effect. *"Much worse."*

33

The police department is buzzing for this time of night. I'm waiting in a room with cinder block walls, a closed-circuit TV, and two hungry, wired kids slamming granola bars and juice boxes like their lives depend on it while I go over the instructions Lucinda gave me before we left.

My name is Elizabeth Jones. I'm a family friend. I'm from Florida. I'm currently going through a nasty divorce from an abusive man. I don't have any form of ID because my husband took it from me in an attempt to keep me from leaving. My husband is dangerous. We've been staying with the McClindons for safety reasons. It's possible the intruder was connected to my husband in some way.

"Say nothing more, nothing less," she told me.

One of the detectives brought some pens and paper for the kids to doodle on a few minutes ago, but so far they're more interested in snacks and asking fifty thousand questions about what happened tonight.

I'm careful with my answers.

I know from watching *Dateline* and its cousins that these rooms are always monitored, always recorded.

I distract them instead, asking where they want to go next.

Georgiana says Disney World.

Jackson says Toledo.

I ask him why Toledo. He giggles without giving me an answer. I tickle him.

This needs to *feel* normal for my children and *look* normal for the police because there isn't a damn thing about any of this that is.

A detective I've not seen before enters the room with a pad of paper and a phone in her hand. She asks if it's okay if the kids hang out with a social worker while we talk. She makes it sound so casual, like it's no big deal or she's doing me a favor, but the idea of letting them go with a stranger who wields the power to take them away sends a shock of heat through my core.

Regardless, I fix my mask, smile, nod, and cooperate. I don't have a choice.

"It won't take long," she tells me with a convincing smile.

"Go with the nice lady," I tell the kids. "I'll be with you soon, okay?"

It's the only lie I've ever told them that I, myself, desperately need to believe.

34

The morning after the police interviews feels strangely peaceful. The five of us eat breakfast in passive quietude, save from clinking bowls, dragging spoons, and the occasional scrape of chairs—but at least we're here.

I was certain last night would be *it*.

I thought there was no way they'd buy the story Lucinda gave me about being Elizabeth Jones from Florida. I figured they'd see the botched hair and the two kids and surely someone would put it all together.

But we walked out of there, free as doves.

Zoey's stare is extra cold and sharp this morning. I think of the way she looked after shooting Evan last night. She might as well have swatted a gnat. Zero remorse. Zero afterthought. And now she's sitting right beside my sweet, innocent son.

We have more in common than I'd like to admit.

I tap my nails against the table, the sound a metronome for my thoughts.

Before we left for the police department last night, the three of us discussed our stories of how the night unfolded, making sure they were lined up with surgical precision. We agreed to suggest that the "intruder" was either the same local creep breaking into neighborhood houses . . . or a deranged man sent by my estranged husband. We agreed my life was in danger—because it was. And we agreed Zoey was scared for all of our lives and did what she had to do.

It feels like we're three literal partners in crime.

The children ask if they can swim today. Their voices are soft, tentative, but the plea is in their eyes. We've been cooped up for days and after last night, they need an outlet for their energy.

I nod. "After breakfast."

"When is Daddy coming?" Jack asks between bites of jelly toast.

Lucinda doesn't look up.

Zoey stares at her phone.

It's as if no one heard the question—or they're ignoring it.

"I'm not sure, sweetheart," I say.

"He said it would be soon," my son says with a pout, still insisting he spoke with Will on the phone. "That's what he told me. I miss him."

Still no reaction from Zoey or Lucinda.

"I'll let you know as soon as *I* know," I tell him. The answer doesn't appear to satisfy him completely, but he stops asking.

The morning air is humid against my skin after breakfast. The kids dive into the pool one by one. I settle onto a lounge chair, pull out my phone, and scroll the local news outlets.

Local Man Killed in Affluent Chicago Suburb Home

Authorities responded late last night to a reported break-in at a residence in [redacted]. One man is confirmed dead. His identity has not been released pending notification of next of kin. Police say the incident is an active, ongoing investigation.

No names. No context. No real details. Nothing about what really happened.

This is a good thing.

I keep thinking of his words, how he accused me of "ruining his family."

And then I think of Zoey telling me Evan was her "real" dad.

Next I think about how easy it was for Lucinda to convince Zoey to participate in the murder of her own biological father—lunatic or not.

After a while longer, my mind wanders to Lucinda and her strangely heroic actions. This woman has spent her entire life hating and torturing me—only to save my kids and protect me from prison?

Nothing adds up.

And deep down I know, this isn't over yet.

Far from it.

35

Lucinda went shopping today for a funeral dress, and I couldn't be more grateful for the break. We've been spending too much time together lately. Every minute with her becomes more confusing and begs more questions that'll never get answered because *everyone lies here*.

I've thought all morning about leaving. It'd be easy to do, knowing Lucinda's occupied. But the money issue remains. And with Will still looking for me, I have to take extra precautions—precautions I might not be able to afford to do.

I'm seated across from Zoey in the kitchen, who's already slouched in her chair like she's bored with me before I've even opened my mouth. Her AirPods look like ornaments, one in, one loosely placed, the soundtrack of her own private theater always running in the background.

"So what's your plan?" I ask softly, tilting my head as if I'm just curious, as if this isn't a noose tightening.

Her lips curl into a sly little smile. "Plan?"

I pitch forward like I'm sharing a secret. "You know, Evan told me he was here to protect *you* from *Lucinda*. Then she turned around and had you kill him. All of this after Rob was poisoned. She's protecting me. But what about you? You're not worried she'll pin your father's death on you?"

Zoey's smirk disappears, but her eyes glint. "You're the one that needs money. You're the one who'd benefit the most from Lucinda inheriting my father's estate."

God damnit.

She's not wrong.

Is this why Lucinda wanted to keep Evan from killing me? So she could frame me for Rob's murder?

"Amateur." She rolls her eyes.

Her theory soaks into my marrow, deep in my bones, growing heavier with each passing thought.

"Why do you think she's protecting you?" Zoey stares at her phone but she's speaking to me. "Ever ask yourself that?"

"Million-dollar question."

She lifts a shoulder. "Just something to think about."

"What's in this for you? Trying to scare me or something?"

"Just giving you some food for thought," she says, "sister to sister."

I squint. Her words come off like a confident threat or rage-bait. Either way, I don't trust her any more or less than I trust Lucinda, and that's saying something.

"Rob—*Dad*—loved my mom or maybe he just loved the way she made him feel, but I don't think he ever really trusted her. When I came along, he had his will rewritten. Made me the sole beneficiary of everything with the secondary beneficiary being his sister in Rhode Island," she says. "Suddenly it wasn't as simple as kill-Rob-inherit-money. It was . . . all the money belongs to Zoey."

Pieces start to pull together in a way that, for once, makes sense. Was that the real reason Evan was so worried about Zoey? Because if there was no Zoey, there would be no inheritance.

Assuming this is all true, of course.

I don't know that it is.

But it's not implausible.

"Mom has more of a reason to protect me than you is all I'm getting at," she says. "She's not going to pin my dad's death on me because she knows she'd never see a dime of that money and all of this would've been for nothing."

I exhale, loud, resigned, loathing the fact that she's onto something.

Zoey cocks her chin down. "You still haven't thanked me for saving your life, by the way."

"Thank you."

She offers a pleased grin that might as well mean nothing because people like her—like *us*—don't feel pleasure, not in a traditional sense.

"You said asking for money could be used against me," I say, thinking about her words a bit more. "But you don't think being the sole heir to a massive estate implicates you in any of this?"

She fixes me with a look too taciturn for her age. "I'm thirteen. A year ago, I was a literal child. How could I mastermind something like this? I don't even know what a *will* is."

The way she says all of this, the tilt of her chin, the calm steadiness of her gaze—it isn't just a performance.

It's a flex.

There's a chance Zoey could be Lucinda incarnate, only compressed into a younger, sharper body.

I soften my face and play the angle that's kept me in the game this long.

"Sorry," I say, resigned. "I'm not trying to argue with you, just examining this from all angles. Lucinda is a mastermind. She's always going to be ten steps ahead of us."

She stares at me, her expression unreadable.

Then her phone rings.

She saunters confidently out of the room, sliding her earbuds back into place, her voice already switching to a light, cheerful tone as she answers what sounds like a call from a friend.

In this moment, I realize, bone chillingly, that I've underestimated Zoey from the very beginning.

Every unsettling little thing—the notes, the footsteps, the knife—suddenly rearranges itself in my mind, not as accidents or Lucinda's schemes or Evan's creepiness . . . but as parts of Zoey's plan.

If I've traded one monster for another, at least it's a familiar monster. One that I know—maybe even better than she knows herself.

36

The morning of Rob's funeral drags, long and brittle, every passing minute snapping like dry twigs underfoot. Lucinda flits from room to room with her grief mask perfectly affixed, murmuring into the phone each time it rings, accepting pity like a stripper desperate to catch floating dollar bills, playing the widow who has lost everything but still manages to be radiantly beautiful despite her sorrow.

My children cling to me, restless but quiet. I reminded them earlier that this is a "sad" day.

But Zoey's the one I'm watching the most, the way she drifts through the house like smoke—here, then gone, impossible to grasp, invisibly lingering.

By late morning, I corner her in the upstairs hall. No witnesses, no Lucinda hovering to snatch her back into orbit. Just the two of us.

If she were a "normal" kid, I wouldn't be doing this on the day of her father's funeral, but after our conversation yesterday and everything that's come to light, I'm confident this kind of talk won't faze her.

"Are you one hundred percent positive she'll protect you?" I ask, my voice subdued but dangerous in its calm. I'm planting seeds of doubt, chipping at that confidence she wore like a princess crown yesterday.

Zoey blinks at me, curious. "What are you talking about?"

"I overheard Lucinda on the phone earlier," I lie. "Something about a toxicology report coming in soon."

I step closer. Zoey's body stiffens and her jaw tightens, though her expression stays ice cold.

"If things turn ugly, if the police start asking harder questions or doing more digging, who do you think she'll sacrifice? If she tells the truth about me, my identity, she'll be branded a liar. Every interview she gave will be thrown out, useless. But you? You're thirteen. A kid. No judge is going to prosecute you, not in any real way. A slap on the wrist, maybe a rehabilitation program or some kind of juvenile detention. You're the perfect scapegoat. Don't you see?"

Zoey's mouth opens, then shuts. Her eyes flash but she doesn't speak. She's silent, unmoving, but I can tell behind those eyes she's digesting my words. Yesterday's confidence is nowhere to be found.

"She uses everyone. Everyone. She promised to kill me once. That's the real reason I left. Then she conspired with Evan to kill Rob. And *you* think *you're* different? Special?" My laugh is sharp, bitter. "You're not special. You're a tool. A pawn. A throwaway. Someone she can use until she doesn't need you anymore. Just like the rest of us."

Zoey's lips press tight but her quietude is loud.

"Tell me," I press, softer now, almost kind. "What has she ever done to make you feel like you mean anything to her?"

"I already told you." She straightens her shoulders. "Dad left everything to me."

"Are you sure? Because the other week, Lucinda mentioned Rob told her he was going to change his will . . . something about wanting to make sure the two of you were taken care of. It was when he was in the hospital." I lean in. "You know . . . when she wouldn't let you visit him."

The hall stays still, the air heavy. Zoey says nothing, but her eyes remain planted on mine. I let her discomfort bloom, then turn and walk off, leaving her alone with the seeds I've planted. It won't be long before they start germinating.

For the first time in days, satisfaction warms my chest.

I won't call this a victory, not yet—but it's leverage.

And under this roof? Leverage is survival.

37

By the time Lucinda and Zoey were ready to leave this morning, the house smelled of hair spray, ironed clothes, and perfume layered on too thick. The two of them were talking in Zoey's room, her door cracked a couple of inches, enough to let Lucinda's voice carry down the hall.

"You have to be on your best behavior today. Do you understand me? For once in your life, Zoey, don't make me regret bringing you." It was the first time in days Lucinda didn't sound like a grieving country club widow.

"Why? He's dead. Everyone grieves differently." Zoey's reply was flat, adolescent acid. Typical thirteen-year-old, personality disorder or not.

There was a slap of silence after that, and I imagine it stung worse than if Lucinda had actually hit her.

"People will be watching both of us," Lucinda hissed. "And I know you can turn on the tears. You do it all the time."

The wedge was there, splitting wood grain, just as I wanted.

I spent the rest of the day basking in the smug satisfaction that my seeds are, in fact, germinating. With those two at odds, with whatever's truly going on, maybe they won't team up against me.

When Lucinda and Zoey return at the end of the day, both dressed in black, Lucinda still sleek and polished, I can't help but notice Zoey looking sullen and slouched, her eyeliner smudged like war paint—proof she cried.

She gave Lucinda what Lucinda wanted.

My satisfaction withers until I pick up on the tension between them, thick and undeniable. Neither of them look at me, but they don't look at each other either. They retreat to their respective rooms upstairs. Zoey slams her door. Lucinda locks hers.

The house is still when the knock at the front door echoes through the foyer.

It isn't the sharp *tap-tap-tap* of a neighbor or the heavy pounding of uniformed officers that's become a mainstay around here lately. I ignore it at first. Then they knock again, louder this time. Breath held, I open the door to a man in plain clothes and a badge in his hand.

"Mrs. McClindon?" His voice is calm but threaded with steel. He has kind, intelligent eyes, rough hands, cropped hair, and threads of gray in his temples. Nice at first glance but not the type of man who's easily pushed around. "I'm Detective Webber."

Every nerve in my body bristles, but I smooth my features into something serene. I don't say "yes" and I know better than to ask how I can help him. The person who says the least always wins—except I'm not sure what kind of game we're playing.

I've stared down worse men than him. But now, with Evan's blood still ghosting the corners of this house, with Will still out there somewhere, with Zoey's poisonous arrogance burned into my brain, the floor tilts beneath me.

I swallow hard, force my throat to loosen.

"Toxicology just came in, and I've been assigned to your husband's case. Was wondering if you wouldn't mind coming down to the station," he says with a smile I don't trust. "Routine questioning."

"I'm not Mrs. McClindon." I brace myself, hoping he doesn't ask who I am, though if he did, I'd tell him Elizabeth Jones. "She's upstairs, resting. She buried her husband today."

Inside, I feel the roll of nausea, hot and sharp. Things are about to unfold in ways no one can predict . . . except maybe Lucinda, the conductor of this orchestra.

His gray-brown brows lift. "Ah, okay. My sincere apologies. I was not made aware that that was today."

He loiters for a second, eyes diverted and brows furrowed as he thinks.

I glance at my children in the living room behind me—heads bent over their crayons, innocent, oblivious.

Detective Webber fishes a card out of his wallet and hands it over. "If you could let her know I stopped by, I'd appreciate it. I'll be back tomorrow."

"Of course," I say, before shutting the door and quietly locking it.

When I'd planted those seeds earlier with Zoey, I was mostly bullshitting her, trying to instill a bit of fear into her. The scenario I posed wasn't unlikely; in fact, it was inevitable.

I just didn't expect it to happen so soon.

38

I accompany Lucinda to the station the next day, mostly as an insurance policy. The place smells like burnt coffee, disinfectant, and the sweat of too many lies. It's the kind of place where the truth doesn't live, only fluorescent lit versions of it.

They guide us down a hallway that echoes with every step. The walls are a pale yellow, meant to soothe, but the random smudges and handprints mixed in make my skin crawl. I imagine people being dragged out, crying, wailing, contorting, desperately grabbing at the cinder block walls but there's nothing to hold on to.

Freedom is something we all take for granted.

We never think about it until it's taken away.

Detective Webber is polite but deliberate, his body language intentionally neutral, like he's just here to piece together a puzzle.

He opens the door to a small interview room and gestures her inside before telling her he'll be right back after he sets the kids and me up in his office.

She turns to look at me, and for the first time ever, there appears to be a silent plea in her eyes . . . a wordless *help*.

Behind her, the table is bolted to the floor. Two chairs, a pitcher of water, a camera in the corner, blinking red. If I cared about this woman, I'd have told her the trick is to look nervous but not too nervous. Vulnerable but not unstable. A woman who's been pushed too far but still deserves sympathy.

Unfortunately for her, I do not care about her.

I wish I did.

I wish I could.

I wish we were a typical mother and daughter, the ones who fight hard only to make up harder, the ones who have each other's backs come hell or high water.

But we're not.

Webber gets us set up in his office, cheap, waxy crayons and police-themed coloring books for the kids who have boredom in their eyes before they so much as sit down.

He shuts the door behind him when he leaves, and we settle in. I grab my phone to scroll news sites for the latest updates. Since Evan died, no one's been posting any Chicago sightings of the kids and me. It's not proof that it was him, but it's worth noting.

"Hey, I was using red," Jackson whines when Georgiana steals his crayon.

He jerks it out of her hand, bumping Webber's computer mouse in the process. The screen of his desktop computer flashes to life, showing Webber and Lucinda in the interview room.

He left the closed-circuit software up?

The two are gesturing back and forth, but there's no sound.

I reach for the keyboard, searching for the volume keys, hardly able to tap them fast enough.

I keep the volume low—enough for me to hear—and inch closer to the speakers. I don't want the kids to hear any of this.

"Mrs. McClindon," he says, settling across from her. "I appreciate you coming in, and I'm very sorry about the loss of your husband. The department thought very highly of him, and we offer you our deepest condolences. Only reason you're here today is because toxicology came back, and I just wanted to clarify a few things."

She nods, leaning forward slightly, as if she's eager to help. "Of course."

"Why don't you start from the beginning?" he says, clicking his pen and pressing the tip against a yellow legal pad. "Tell me what happened the night your husband passed away, in your own words."

She takes a slow breath, her lower lip quivering.

"It was just a normal night," she says, taking her time, staring to the side, at nothing. "My husband said he wanted to get a few things done in his study before bed . . . he did that sometimes . . . I didn't think anything of it until I woke up sometime around midnight and realized he hadn't come to bed. I went downstairs and found him still in his study . . . slumped over his desk."

The waterworks begin to fall.

Webber hands her a tissue.

"That must've been difficult to see," he says, offering empty words of comfort.

"Rob was the love of my life," she tells him between sobs, her delivery compelling. "Fourteen years wasn't enough time with him."

The detective's pen drags slowly across the page before coming to a hard stop.

"I can't imagine," he says, like he knows anything about that. "But here's the thing, Mrs. McClindon. Your husband's toxicology came back and something was flagged."

Her face becomes a sheet of white.

"Did anyone else interact with him in the hours leading up to his passing?" he asks, no longer beating around the bush with hollow sympathy.

"Our house guest," she says without hesitation.

He peers over his glasses at her. "Is that the woman who answered the door last night? The one who drove you here tonight?"

Lucinda gently blows her nose, nodding. "She's having a bit of a difficult time right now, going through a divorce, so she's been staying with us. We were helping her get on her feet."

I swallow hard, already knowing how this is going to go.

She's going to paint me as troubled, money-hungry, unstable, and murderous.

Zoey was right.

My fists clench until my nails dig deep into my palms, nearly breaking the skin.

I barely feel it.

"And what's your house guest's name?" he asks, pen ready.

My heart ricochets in my chest. This is her chance to do it, to throw me under the bus. It'd be risky of her to lie, but Lucinda's taken calculated risks her entire life. Why stop now?

Webber leans back in his chair, patiently waiting for her response.

"Elizabeth," Lucinda says.

I exhale.

Why is she still protecting me? What's her angle?

"Do you have any reason to believe your house guest would've wanted to harm your husband?" Webber asks.

"No," Lucinda says with conviction and without pause. "Not to my knowledge. But my daughter, Zoey, was quite close with him. They were always together." She offers a bittersweet half smile. "To be honest, sometimes I felt like the third wheel with those two. But I was just happy Zoey had a good father who loved her. That's all a mother could ask for, you know?"

Oxygen returns to my lungs.

The walls stop closing in.

Still, I'm struggling to wrap my head around what's happening versus what I thought was about to happen . . .

Lucinda is crafting a narrative that absolves me and sets up the possibility that Zoey had been poisoning her father.

She's actually throwing her child under the bus, like I predicted she would.

Zoey wasn't right . . . *I* was.

Webber studies her for a lengthy moment, then leans forward. "You understand, we'll need to corroborate some of these details. I'll need to interview both your daughter and your house guest."

"You think . . ." She lets her voice evaporate. "You think one of them did something to Rob?"

He closes his notebook, slides it to the side. "I don't know what to think yet, but it appears someone did. Based on the toxicology findings, there was an unusual substance in his system. I'm not yet at liberty to say what that was. But what I can share is we're opening a homicide investigation."

My breath hitches.

Lucinda leans back in her chair, slow and dramatic, lifting her fingertips to her lips and letting them tremble just so. "I just . . . I'm sorry . . . this is a lot to take in. I don't . . . there's no way . . . no . . ."

Webber observes her for another long moment, then stands. "I appreciate you coming down tonight. That's all I need for now. I'd love to interview Zoey tomorrow."

I scramble to my feet, tapping down the volume and turning off the computer monitor until it's nothing but a black screen.

A minute later, Webber returns with Lucinda and asks if I have time to answer a few questions.

I maintain every detail of Lucinda's story, confirming that my name is Elizabeth, that I'm a house guest, that I'd not been around Rob the night of his death, that I was going through some marital difficulties, that Zoey and Rob were close, but I didn't find it unusual. When he asks for a photo ID, I tell him my estranged husband stole it from me in an attempt to keep me from leaving—same thing I told the detective the night of Evan's murder.

My answers appear to satisfy him.

I realize, walking out of that station into the strange warm glow of morning sun with Lucinda and my children in tow, that I've never been less alone.

Evil is on my side.

And I'm not sure how I feel about that.

39

The drive back from the station is a surreal blur of blinding daylight, the sun splintering through the windshield like we're hurtling through a tunnel of glass.

My palms are slick against the steering wheel, the radio a faint murmur that might as well be a foreign language as I replay the interview in my head. By the time Lucinda's massive brick estate—a monument to her capabilities—comes into view, the sight of it makes my stomach twist.

I park in the driveway this time and sit there for a beat too long, gripping the wheel, staring at the wide front windows like they might blink at me.

Jackson brought up Will again last night before bed.

He won't stop insisting they spoke on the phone. In fact, he gets angry when I try to shut it down. Kids say things all the time then let them go or forget about them and move on. But he's yet to let this go.

"Would you mind if I started parking in the garage?" I ask Lucinda.

"Not at all, sweetheart. I'll get you an opener." She climbs out of the car, heads inside, and returns with a small gray remote with four buttons. "You can have the stall on the very right."

Her kindness is attached with all kinds of invisible strings, I'm sure of it. But in case anyone has seen us out and about today, in case Will truly is close . . . I need to keep my car hidden.

When we finally step inside the house, the air is thick, motionless. And there she is. Zoey, standing in the hallway, her face drawn, her eyes dark hollows that reveal nothing. For the longest stretch, we stare at each other, the tension between us sharp enough to slice.

"Where were you guys?" she asks.

"We met with a detective. He had some questions," Lucinda tells her, placing a hand on her shoulder as if the act is some kind of reassurance.

"About *what*?" Zoey's question comes off as a paranoid demand.

"Apparently they're looking into your father's death," Lucinda says.

"Why were you guys gone so long?" Zoey jerks her shoulder away.

Lucinda shrugs. "He had a lot of questions."

"What'd he ask?" Zoey follows our mother through the kitchen.

"The same ones he's probably going to ask you," I say. "The detective wants to meet with you tomorrow."

I spot no reaction or response from her, not at first glance, but then I notice something brewing behind those dead blue eyes. Zoey's normally a fortress of unreadable expression, yet today something's beginning to fray at the edges.

"Why didn't you just take me with you today?" she asks. Her question is innocent at surface level, but we all know it's pointed.

"He didn't ask to see you," Lucinda answers. "Just me."

Zoey folds her arms. "Why'd Camille go?"

"Why so many questions?" Lucinda sniffs a laugh through her nose, like it amuses her to see her child so wound up.

"So what's this have to do with me? Why do they want to interview me?" Her arms cross tighter, her tone growing defensive.

Lucinda sighs. "Zoey, I spent the last hour answering questions. I don't feel like spending another hour doing it all over again. My head is pounding. I'm going to lie down upstairs."

"Mommy, we wanna swim." Jackson tugs on my sleeve.

Turning to Zoey, I offer an apology. "It's been a long day for them. We're going to soak up the sun while we still can. You're welcome to join?"

If looks could kill, I'd be dead right now. "Why are you being so casual about this?"

I squint, feigning confusion. "Should I not be? I think the more important question is . . . why are you not?"

She takes a step back, and I gather my kids and head to the staircase in the foyer.

"I didn't do anything," she calls after me. Footsteps follow next. In a matter of seconds, she's running up the stairs behind us. "Are you two trying to pin something on me?"

There it is.

The seed that germinated yesterday is beginning to sprout.

She thinks Lucinda and I are in cahoots—a theory as laughable as it is . . . sort of true.

Not by choice.

If it were up to me, I'd have nothing to do with any of this.

I simply refuse to go down for something I didn't do.

Her energy is dense with paranoia and uncertainty. I stop, turning back to look at her, relishing for a moment in how small and young and scared she looks.

For a second, I almost believe her.

But deep down, I know better.

40

The next day, the kitchen is so full of food and flowers you can barely see the counters. Lasagnas in foil pans, platters of sandwiches, casseroles with handwritten reheating instructions taped to their lids. Arrangements of lilies and white roses and sunflowers shoved into every available vase, their perfume warring with the smell of meat and starch. Visitors come in shifts, a rotation of mourners and well-wishers, each bringing condolences like offerings to a shrine. Lucinda laps it up like a kitten to milk, keeping her claws meticulously retracted.

I stay hidden upstairs, with the kids.

No one knows we're here—except the local police.

It needs to stay that way.

By afternoon, a copy of the *Daily Suburban Times* is splayed out on the counter. The headline stretches across the page in bold black ink. Above the sprawling article is a photograph of Lucinda, dressed in head-to-toe black, a veil and everything, sobbing over Rob's casket before it's lowered into the ground.

LOCAL FAMILY SHAKEN BY ANOTHER TRAGEDY; COMMUNITY RALLIES BEHIND THEM

In a shocking incident that has left a quiet community reeling, prominent businessman Robert McClindon was laid to rest this week following what authorities are calling an "intrusion turned deadly." Police say the shooting victim was Evan Anthony Wheeler, a local man believed to have been squatting in the unfinished apartment above the McClindon family's garage.

Despite the harrowing circumstances, Mrs. Lucinda McClindon has displayed remarkable grace, hosting friends and family in her home and demonstrating strength in the face of one of the town's greatest tragedies.

"Lucinda McClindon is the heart and soul of this community," one neighbor told reporters. "Even in grief, she thinks of others first."

Authorities have not released the name of the person who fatally shot Evan Wheeler, citing the ongoing investigation.

I turn on the television, desperate for distraction, and land on a national news segment. My blood runs cold when I see a familiar face—one I never thought I'd see again because I thought she was dead.

Sozi . . . the neighbor whose lifeless body I'd found in our Phoenix garage, the body that disappeared hours later and subsequently led to Will blackmailing me into staying . . . is alive, well, and apparently giving a plethora of interviews about Will's lying, cheating, manipulating ways.

I grab the remote and dial up the volume, unable to take my eyes off the screen.

According to Sozi, the two had been having an affair for years—news to me—and he promised that if she helped him, he'd finally leave me and be with her forever. It's a tale as old as time and she's definitely dumb enough to believe it, but my God her timing couldn't have been better.

After discrediting Will, she goes on to speak about my character, how I was the "perfect" mother and a "loving" wife, that there was nothing "crazy" about me like Will's saying.

No shit.

At one point, she looks straight at the camera and says, "Camille, if you're watching, wherever you are, I'm so sorry, and I hope you and the kids can come home soon. You don't deserve what I did to you—or what Will did to you."

If she hadn't been screwing my husband behind my back for years, I'd kiss the screen right now.

"Will Prescott is a manipulator," she goes on to say to the interviewer. Her voice is firm, brimming with indignation. "He lied to me. He convinced me to set up his wife—he told me Camille was dangerous, unstable, that she had a history of mental illness. He made me believe I was doing the right thing by helping him. He convinced me I was helping the kids. After a while, I realized things weren't adding up. And Will was . . . not who I thought he was. That's when I left him. Once I realized what he was capable of, I couldn't stay."

The reporter leans forward. "Can you elaborate more on what it was that made you reach this conclusion?"

Sozi nods, a small, practiced smile. "I'll be sharing everything in my book. The truth deserves to be told. This isn't just a story about a woman being manipulated—it's about a man who spun an entire web of lies to trap people in his orbit. It's darker, stranger, more unbelievable than anything you could imagine. Men like this are everywhere, hiding in plain sight. If my story helps even one woman avoid getting involved with someone like that . . ."

A shiver runs down my arms, leaving a path of hairs standing on end.

Part of me is glad Sozi's writing a tell-all. Will deserves to be painted for what he is: a handsome, charming, devious monster.

But on the other hand, my stomach twists at the thought of my children watching their father dissected on prime-time news and in the mainstream media, their classmates whispering about the book their father inspired. They'll grow up in the shadow of his sins, tainted by blood they didn't ask for. Descendants of a man whose legacy is abhorrent.

I mute the television, staring at the frozen image of Sozi's righteous face until my burning eyes force me to blink.

Before I can think another thought, Lucinda's expensive perfume fills the room. Behind me, she collapses onto the sofa with a graceful sigh, her onyx cashmere pashmina wrapping around her like fine couture.

She leans her head back and closes her eyes.

"I've had enough people for today," she murmurs, pressing her hand to her forehead. "If anyone else stops by, could you kindly turn them away?"

Her tone is airy, but it lands like an order. She wants me to play butler—which means risking exposing myself even more. Irritation rises in me hot and fast, but I swallow it down.

I'm not in a position to say no.

I still need to ask her for money.

Evan, obviously, never came through for me—not that he was ever going to. The man clearly had other plans.

"Sure." I sip my coffee, watching her. Before I leave, I switch the TV off. I never told her about Sozi, about the dead neighbor I believed Will killed to blackmail me. I didn't want to complicate an already complicated situation, nor did I want to give Lucinda any potential ammunition to use against me. "Does Zoey seem okay to you today? She was acting a little strange earlier. Have you talked to her?"

Lucinda's eyes open, bright and glistening, and she smiles at me. Menacing. Serene. "I just buried my husband two days ago, Camille. Can we not discuss this right now?"

Her mask has slipped, revealing a fact I already knew—she couldn't care less about Zoey.

"I just want to make sure she's okay. There was an article about the shooting in the paper. They didn't name the shooter, but it's only a matter of time—"

"Zoey's fine." She tilts her head. "She's *always* fine."

"When are you taking her to see Detective Webber?" I ask.

She blows an annoyed puff of air through her lips. "Obviously not today."

"I feel like Will is close," I say, taking the opportunity to change the subject. "I keep thinking we need to get out of here. Everyone talks, a lot of people have seen me here, the police know I'm here . . ."

"They think your name is Elizabeth. No one's pieced anything together, and they won't."

Lucinda pinches the narrow bridge of her nose. "Besides, where are you going to go?"

"I'm not sure. I don't have a lot of money, so that limits my options."

"It costs you nothing to live here."

"I can't live here forever . . ." I say gently, so as not to risk offending her. "I really appreciate everything you've done for us. Truly. But people online have posted that we're in the Chicago area. It's only a matter of time before Will finds us. And you've been through so much this past week. I don't want to—"

"Stop." She cuts me off, lifting a palm. "You're safer here than you'll be anywhere else. If that pompous idiot wants to come for you and the children, he'll have to get through me first, and you and I both know how that'll go."

Her voice is honey laced with venom, a frequency people can hear only if they're attuned to it.

I'm at an extraordinary loss for words trying to wrap my head around how to get us out of this situation.

What's her endgame? Because Lucinda *always* has one.

"Jackie keeps insisting she talked to Will on the phone last week," I say.

"Can we please stop referring to your son as she?" Lucinda's words slice like one of her freshly sharpened kitchen knives.

How long has she known? And how did she know?

And why didn't she say something sooner?

I clench my fist in frustration—at both Lucinda and myself.

What else does she know that she hasn't let on about?

I think back to a handful of times when they'd be coloring or drawing, Georgie would use pinks and purples and draw rainbows and Jackson would use greens and blues and draw stick figures and dinosaurs. Or that one afternoon when Georgie wanted to play "mermaids" in the pool. Little moments like that reappear in my mind, all of them nuanced. I didn't think Lucinda noticed given her constant state of self-absorption, but obviously that's not the case.

"I get the reason behind it, I understand why you disguised them, but it's not necessary here," she adds. "With me. They can be who they are here. And so can you. I need to rest now."

With that, she gets up and heads to her room, leaving me just as destitute as I was when I arrived.

41

Zoey and I sit across from each other at the far end of the kitchen island like opponent pieces in a quiet game. The house finally asleep after the daylong parade—empty casserole dishes stacked in the sink, flowers wilting just a shade, sympathy cards arranged as if they could absorb sound.

Lucinda took a sleeping pill an hour ago.

The kids are passed out in our guest suite.

It's just us.

She somehow appears older than she did yesterday, as if every minute of the last twenty-four hours found a place to live on her face. She rests her forearms on the counter and stares at her hands before fidgeting with her AirPods, then tapping and swiping on her phone screen. I'm not convinced she's doing anything but going through motions.

"You should probably eat." I haven't seen her touch a morsel of food all day. She's got to be starving.

Her sunken gaze flicks to mine and she smirks. "What are you, my mother?"

"No, thank God."

We both laugh.

It's a strange thing to bond over, being the progeny of Lucinda, but here we are.

"You doing okay?" I ask when she seems more malleable and receptive.

"You don't have to pretend to care."

"I wouldn't ask if I didn't."

My response satisfies her enough that she offers me a shrug and a tight half smile. "It's just a weird time. And Lucinda's theatrics are getting old."

"At least we get a break from her tonight." I glance at the clock above the stove. It's barely past eight. "Thank God for Ambien."

"I don't think you should leave," she says.

I study her before I ask why.

"I don't want to be alone with Lucinda," she answers.

"You didn't seem worried about her before. What changed?"

"She's nicer when you're around."

"I've noticed," I say. "This is definitely not the same person who used to feed me raw hamburger."

"You can't leave me with her."

"Zoey, I can't stay." I exhale. "My husband's looking for us. He's going to show up here any day, and it's going to put all of us in danger."

"I kept you safe from Evan. I'll keep you safe from Will, too."

A quiet falls, almost companionable. She looks over my shoulder toward the window behind me, at the black reflection of glass where we're both faint ghosts.

"Take me with you," she says.

"I wish I could. I can't risk it. You're safer here." I lie through my teeth, but isn't that what we do? Isn't that what everyone does here?

"I've watched some of his interviews. He seems very convincing," she says. "But I can see through it. It's an act."

"He's not a good person. And he's very angry right now. I don't trust him not to do something awful to me or anyone who stands in his way."

"Why are you talking to me like I'm just a kid? Did you not see me shoot Evan?"

"Zoey, you *are* just a kid," I say. "A very mature one, but still. And of course I saw you shoot Evan."

"I'll shoot Will, too. If you want," she says without hesitation. "Maybe we can bait him, set him up, and when he gets here, we'll make it look like he was about to attack—"

I lift a hand, stopping her right there. "We're not conspiring to murder my husband. And the last thing you need is a second self-defense murder on your rap sheet."

I just want to get my children out of here and raise them in some semblance of safety and normalcy.

"So what's *your* plan, then?" she asks.

"It's private."

"You don't trust me enough to tell me." It's more of a statement than a question.

"You've not really given me reason to."

She absorbs this, and something like respect shifts across her face. Or perhaps it's hunger for approval. I'm getting tired, it's been a long, exhausting day.

"We should both try to sleep," I say.

She nods, small as a child agreeing to brush her teeth. Then she stands, pushing back the barstool. "You should know, you're making a really dumb mistake."

"What do you mean?"

"Not trusting me," she says. "Like you said, we could be an unstoppable force together . . . or each other's worst enemies. You said it was my choice. I made mine. What's yours?"

"Give me a reason to trust you," I tell her. "And I will."

"I saved your life. Is that not enough?"

"Lucinda saved my children's lives. That still doesn't make me trust her."

"What's it going to take?" she asks.

"Time."

Time we don't have . . .

Jamming her AirPods tighter into place, she huffs, tromping upstairs.

I follow.

She takes the left staircase. I take the right. We meet at the top and go our own ways.

In my bedroom, I tuck the children in again, though they're still asleep. Georgie murmurs, Jackson's fingers curl around my thumb for a second and then loosen. I check their AirTags the way some mothers check nightlights. I kiss their foreheads and breathe them in like it's an antidote for all the craziness we've been through lately, and it sort of is.

Then I sit in the chair by the window and attempt to plot our exit. The other day, while they were at the funeral, I considered scouring the house for antiques and valuables—then I thought of the cameras in every corner. Lucinda would be furious if I stole from her and left without her "permission," and she'd find a way to make all of this ten times worse for me than it already is.

Restless, I peek my head out the door, glancing into the hallway for lack of something better to do. I just need to move. Exhaustion gnaws my bones, but sitting still makes them ache.

From the corner of my eye, in the seconds before I close my bedroom door, I catch a hint of blue light coming from under the garage apartment door.

The police already did their investigation after Evan's death, concluding he was squatting unbeknownst to anyone, just like Lucinda claimed. They hauled away piles of evidence and random things proving he was squatting. They took a million photos. They were thorough. Lucinda shut off the lights and latched the door afterward. I watched her.

No one would have any reason to go in there.

And why would anyone want to?

The place was filthy, disgusting, and reeked of unwashed bedding and body odor.

My heart hammers so hard, it pulses in my ears.

From here, I can see the dead bolt is latched from this side.

Tiptoeing over, I hold my breath and press my ear against the thick wood, praying I don't hear any signs of life on the other side.

I exhale when I'm met with several minutes of complete silence, and I return to my room.

The children are still where I left them, turned into small parentheses by sleep. I sit beside them on the bed and stare at the dark ceiling and make a new plan in my head, then a second one in case the first one hemorrhages, then a third plan for when those plans become liabilities.

I stroke Jackson's hair off his forehead and bask in the heat of his little body, the way it steadies my hands. Then I touch Georgie's cheek with the back of my hand, the way my mother never did mine. The room smells like store-brand shampoo and the faint dust that floats inside lamplight, even when the lamp is off.

I tell myself I can sleep now.

But I know I won't.

When the floorboard in the hall outside gives a soft complaint—the board by the thermostat that clicks when anyone heavier than Zoey passes—I sit up straight.

Steps pause.

Steps move on.

They're too light, too practiced to be Will's. The steps pass our door, slow, attentive, like a hand running along spines on a shelf.

Then they stop altogether.

Someone's either standing on the other side of our door, or I'm imagining the whole thing due to stress and sleep deprivation.

I lie back down, my eyes wide open in the dark, physically spent but my mind unable to rest tonight.

My thoughts keep going back to Zoey. If I could feel sympathy, she'd have mine—murdering aside. She's a little monster that Lucinda created. It's not her fault she's the way she is. She doesn't know it doesn't have to be this way. She's just a kid trying to survive the only way she knows how. But before I get too carried away giving her the benefit of the doubt, I bury my thoughts in my thought graveyard with the rest.

I can't trust her.

She might not be the eye of the storm, but she's been part of the weather system all along.

42

By the time the garage door shudders open the following afternoon, my nerves are already stretched taut as piano wire. The children are in the den, coloring at the coffee table, the television murmuring cartoons in the background. I hover by the kitchen sink, scrubbing a dish that doesn't need scrubbing, watching the backyard through the slats of the blinds.

The light under Evan's apartment door was off this morning.

Someone was in there.

And someone left.

Lucinda was out cold last night thanks to her Ambien, and I can't imagine what reason Zoey would have to go in there.

From here, I hear Lucinda's Mercedes sedan gliding into place, sleek and self-assured. When Lucinda treks inside, looking immaculate as always—today in a tailored navy sheath dress, and pearls, she looks more like someone who just stepped out of a boardroom meeting, not someone returning from taking her thirteen-year-old daughter to the police station for questioning.

Beside her, Zoey's in ripped black jeans and an oversized hoodie with the sleeves pushed up to her elbows, earbuds clenched in her fist like medals of discontent. I expected Zoey's outfit to infuriate Lucinda earlier; I even braced myself for the exchange I thought they were going to have on their way out.

Only neither of them said more than two words to each other.

It occurred to me after they left that Lucinda doesn't care if Zoey looks unkempt. In fact, Zoey looking unkempt only adds fuel to the fire that Lucinda's been subtly kindling about Zoey.

"We're still out of orange juice? Seriously?" Zoey slams the fridge shut.

Lucinda ignores her the same way she ignored her outfit earlier. She simply stands there sorting the mail, unbothered. "Zoey, can you join me in the study when you have a second, please?"

Zoey grabs fistfuls of air, annoyed, and storms in that direction.

"Rob always took care of this kind of stuff," Lucinda says to no one. Once she's done sifting through bills, she takes her time making her way to the study.

While the two of them were gone, I watched videos on pickpocketing, then scoured the house—nonchalantly, of course—in search of any valuables I could pawn. But all I could find were random antique decor items that could be worth something but were likely worth nothing.

There was no gold, cash, or jewelry hidden anywhere.

Knowing Lucinda, everything of value is locked away, hidden from plain sight.

She knows I'm low on funds and she's made it clear she wants it to stay that way.

With slow, silent footsteps, I inch toward the foyer and linger outside the closed doors of Rob's study, where Lucinda and Zoey are in the middle of a hushed conversation.

"You *have* to keep your story straight," Lucinda instructs with a no-nonsense tone. "If you falter, even once, the entire thing collapses. There can be *no* holes. I cannot stress that enough."

"I told them exactly what you told me to."

"Zoey, if you're lying to me . . ."

"Why would I lie? You think I *want* to be locked up?"

"Of course not. You wouldn't last two seconds behind bars," Lucinda states the obvious, but it's just a flimsy fear tactic.

"I still don't get why you wouldn't let me have our lawyer there. He would've told me what to say."

The fact that Lucinda purposely avoided having an attorney help Zoey answer the detective's questions is telling. She's setting her up to fail and Zoey's too young to understand that.

"Lawyers imply guilt. I have a plan," Lucinda tells her. "And if you interfere with that plan, it's not going to end well for you."

Her threat must land like a nuclear bomb because Zoey says nothing.

I pad away before the two emerge.

I don't know what's going on, but what I *do* know is that I can't trust either of them.

That and we're leaving tomorrow, during the day, when Lucinda and Zoey are at the estate lawyer's office going over Rob's will.

Money or no money, this has gone on long enough, and Lucinda's conspiring knows no end.

We'd leave tonight after everyone's asleep, but Lucinda never fails to arm the house before she goes to bed. We're locked in. But tomorrow? We'll be free.

Whatever freedom looks like.

43

We're all packed up when Lucinda and Zoey return early from the attorney's office. I expected them to be gone longer than this considering Lucinda mentioned grabbing lunch afterward.

The garage entry door slams.

I crumple the note I'd left on the counter, where I scribbled to Lucinda that I was taking the kids out to grab ice cream and would be back soon.

We were five minutes from freedom.

Five. Minutes.

"I can't believe you did this to me," Zoey's voice cracks the air, except this time it's not sulky. Not performative. *Furious.*

"Zoey, you're a child." Lucinda's answer is arctic. "There are certain things you don't understand."

"I understand inheritance," Zoey says, clipped. "I understand that last I checked, Dad left everything to me—not you."

I think of the night I found Zoey in Rob's study, when Lucinda was at the hospital. She was rifling through drawers but said she was looking for his favorite pen. She must've been looking for his will?

"You had him change it," she says, "didn't you? You waited until he was sick in the hospital, not thinking clearly, drugged up, worried about dying. You knew exactly what you were doing."

"You'll still be well cared for and nothing is going to change for you," Lucinda says, perfectly calm. "You have no concept of the legal exposure involved. How investments work. And inheritance taxes alone—"

"Stop." Zoey's voice is a whip. "Stop talking to me like I'm some stupid kid."

Lucinda sighs, wiping patience across her tone like foundation. "I'm talking to you like this because I'm your *mother* and you are a *kid*. I know you're not stupid. You just don't understand how the world works yet. You wouldn't know what to do with that kind of money. I'm protecting you from yourself."

"You seriously expect me to believe that?" Zoey laughs, empty.

"You're my daughter," Lucinda says, and the sentence is carved so smooth and neutral it has no edges. She's simply stating a fact. "It's my job to protect you."

"Yeah, right. I'm not your daughter. I'm your alibi, your scapegoat." She spits the word like a hard pit from a cherry. "Your pawn."

"Zoey, you know all of this melodrama is wasted on me," Lucinda says with an unnerving amount of calm.

They're still bickering near the garage entrance, unaware I'm a mere ten feet away in the kitchen. I creep into an alcove behind a row of cabinets, lingering in the shadows. I need to hear every word of this exchange, but I don't want to be a liability in whatever Lucinda's scheming.

"Just like your games are wasted on me," Zoey counters.

Lucinda slams her Chanel bag on the kitchen island, eyes wild the way they used to be when I was a kid, the same eyes that sent me bolting for my room. *"I've had enough of your disrespect for today."*

"Shove it up your ass, *Lucinda*." Zoey's use of Lucinda's first name lands like a plate shattering. I flatten myself even more against the wall, as if their broken shards might ricochet in my direction.

"To your room. *Now*." Lucinda's voice drops to something dangerous. "I don't want to see you or hear you the rest of the night."

Zoey stands firm, indignant. "All these years, you made me think we were in it together. You said we had to be careful, that I was special, that it would all make sense someday and it'd be worth it. But now? Now you want me quiet and grateful while you take *everything*."

"Because I'm the one the law recognizes," Lucinda says crisply. "Because I'm the adult. Because I planned and protected—"

"Protected?" Zoey laughs, high and sharp. "You let me scream for hours when I was a baby because the sound made you feel powerful. You broke the nanny's phone when she called her mother for advice. You told me crying was manipulative before I could barely talk." Her breath hitches but she doesn't cry. "You don't protect. You control. You ruin. You've never protected anyone in your life—including your first daughter."

My brows lift with Zoey's words, and I bite away a pleased smirk. I know her enough to know she's not capable of true sympathy for what I went through, but in this case, I don't mind being used as ammo. It's the first time anyone's ever muttered those words to Lucinda, and it's about damn time.

Something hard hits the counter.

Maybe Lucinda slaps her palm against it or she sets down a glass with force.

"You're out of line," she says.

"No. I'm just outside the lines you drew," Zoey counters without pause. "You can't control me. Not anymore."

"Listen to me." Lucinda's tone grows darker, lower. "You're angry. Fine. Be angry. You want to throw a tantrum like a child? Have at it. But do it upstairs, not here. I'm not in the mood and I've got work to do."

"Funny. You never called me a *child* when you needed me to do your dirty work," Zoey says. I can almost hear the thread I pulled days ago unwind inside her. Everything's coming to a head, and whatever happens next isn't going to be pretty.

"I'm going to do you a favor and pretend I didn't hear what you just said," Lucinda says, voice cool. "A few family friends will likely stop by tomorrow, and I don't need you in the background making a fuss. Smile. Accept condolences. Go upstairs when I signal. That is your only job."

"My *job*?" Zoey's voice is crystal clear. "No. Here's my job." A rustle, the soft thud of something set on the desk. Paper? A phone? "This is the folder on my Notes app called 'Insurance.' I've been recording you for months. Years, actually, if you count screenshots and research. You threatening to kill Camille when she was seventeen. You convincing Dad to change the titling on the Florida condo. You telling Evan to scrub the camera time stamps or delete footage every time you poisoned him. You telling me to kill Evan. You coaching me on 'how to look appropriately sad' for the funeral. You're a murderer and your days of telling me what to do are over."

A heavy silence blankets the moment.

This could go a number of ways.

If I could feel fear, I'd be scared for Zoey right now.

Then again, Zoey's probably not even scared—the thought of that alone is terrifying.

"You think screenshots will save you?" Lucinda's voice is unshaken, haughty. "Everyone knows those can be faked. And the law doesn't look kindly on dramatic little girls who think they're detectives. Besides, it's illegal to record people without their permission. If you bring any of that into a courtroom, the first thing they'll do is ask how you got it. They'll ask about illegal access, about wiretapping, about intent. Then they'll ask about the shooting. So help me, Zoey, if you throw me under the bus, don't think for one second I won't take you with me."

"What shooting?" Her question sounds innocent, but we all know it's anything but.

"Oh, sweetheart. You're not as clever as you think you are." Lucinda smiles. I can't see it, but I can hear it. A beat of contempt follows. "You have no idea how this world works."

"Careful," Zoey says, her voice new. "There are a hundred ways I can paint the story."

"Paint it any way you like," Lucinda says. "But you're *thirteen* and you will be handled as such by law enforcement and the legal system.

You'll just be seen as another uncontrollable brat. A compulsive liar. An emotional teenager. That's what you seem to keep forgetting."

"I'm not forgetting anything. I remember everything. I remember you telling me crying is for the weak. I remember you saying Evan was 'useful' but only if you kept him hidden and hungry. I remember you laughing when Dad said he wanted to take me to the lake house he always went to when he was a kid. The way you called him 'sentimental,' like it was a bad thing. I remember every nanny's name, how you fired them when they started seeing too much, and I remember the night you made me practice looking surprised in the mirror." Her breath goes tight. "And I remember what I've done to keep Camille's kids safe under this roof." She pauses, dramatic. "So tell me again I'm a child."

"Darling, darling, darling," Lucinda says, soft as silk. "You *are* a child. *My* child. And I love you. That's why I am not going to let you throw your life away over an emotional outburst. Now go upstairs and wash your face. We'll revisit this when you're able to think straighter. I need you rational."

"Say that again," Zoey says, so calm I have to strain to hear it.

"Rational?" Lucinda repeats, not understanding yet.

"No. Say 'I love you' again."

There's a pause.

"I love you," Lucinda says, and this time it sounds as staged as a cinema kiss. "Why?"

"You've never said that to me before," Zoey says. "I wasn't sure I heard you right. But here's my rationale: If you try to put any of this on Camille, I'm going to the police with everything I've got. I've already made a Dropbox. If anything happens to me, it automatically sends a link to ten of your closest friends, to the police, to the bank, to the attorney's office, and to Chief Whitlock, who you keep calling by his first name like he's your pet poodle. If you don't give me what's rightfully mine and if you throw Camille under the bus for what you did to Dad, you'll burn the only bridge you've ever actually cared about, which is your reputation. Do you hear me?"

"Enough with the threats. You think you're scaring me? You're not. Sweet summer child, you're merely presenting me with a set of options."

"If that's what you want to think, go ahead," Zoey says. I picture her crossing her arms, planting her feet on the ground, and I give her silent kudos for standing up to the monster I spent my entire childhood cowering from because I was raised by fear, not nannies. "That's the only reason you've survived this long. But you miscounted me. I'm not an investment. I'm an heir."

"Correction. You *were* an heir," Lucinda says, brisk again, restoring order by tone. "Your father left everything to me so I could take care of you. It's standard for families with minor children. The spouse inherits everything so they can continue providing."

"It wasn't like that before. *You* made him change it," Zoey says. "You're nothing but a liar and all you do is use everyone. Dad. Evan. Me."

"You're not even a McClindon." Lucinda's voice is laced with arrogance. "Not by blood. Had I not taken matters into my own hands when I found out I was pregnant, we'd be penniless. You should be *thanking* me, instead you're acting like an ungrateful little brat."

Lucinda's steps sound slow across the polished wooden floor, like she's closing the distance with the smell of overpriced audacity.

"Look at me," Lucinda coos. "And listen very carefully."

The floor doesn't creak, which means Zoey isn't backing away. I don't know whether that terrifies me or makes me proud.

"You, Zoey, are not my enemy," Lucinda says, intimate and motherly. "You're the only person I've ever truly cared about. You're a part of me whether you like it or not. It's us against the world. Against the police. Against the internet. The gossipers. The ones who want to take what's ours. You can hate me all you want, but you and I are the same, and our lives are about to become extraordinary."

"No," Zoey says, and this time there's something like mercy in the word. "My life was already extraordinary. And you and I? We're not the same. At all. Not even close."

A small thud—maybe a chair tipping back against the credenza. Then a sudden, hard crack. Not a slap; the sound is wrong. More like ceramic meeting wood.

"Oops," Zoey says. "Your wedding photo fell."

Lucinda inhales. "Clean that up."

"Probably shouldn't. There's broken glass," Zoey says. "And I'm just a child."

Lucinda's breath evens. "You want to test me? Fine. Here's a test. You walk out of this room and behave at dinner, and tomorrow I'll consider your request to meet with the attorney together. You continue this—this adolescent display—and I call your school and have them send your transcripts to that boarding program in Utah we discussed last year."

There it is.

Lucinda's power move.

Her proverbial checkmate.

She used to threaten to send me away all the time. The only difference is back then she couldn't have afforded to. Now? She can send Zoey to any "get straight" program in the world. The worst of the worst if she wanted to—and she would.

"Try it," Zoey says. "I'd love being anywhere as long as you weren't there."

"You don't love anything," Lucinda says with an air of condescension in her words. "Except attention."

Zoey doesn't take the bait.

"You have no idea who I am. What I am. What I'm capable of." Dead certainty enters her voice. "That boarding school's going to be a picnic compared to living with you."

"If that's what you want to believe, fine," Lucinda says with a haughty snort.

In the icy, still air, I can almost make out three different hearts deciding who they'll beat for next. I press a palm to the wall, bracing myself, listening to the woman who created me speak to my half sister with her signature contempt.

It was never personal with Lucinda. I was her burden. Zoey is her pawn. The two of us did nothing wrong, we simply had the misfortune of being born.

Zoey moves first. Footsteps—fast, decisive—toward the door. I step back as the knob turns. The door jerks open and she fills the threshold, cheeks flushed, eyes glassy but dry, mouth pulled into a line so flat it could cut glass. She almost crashes into me but doesn't startle. She looks at me like she already knew I was there.

"You hear what you wanted to hear?" she asks, brows raised.

"I heard enough," I say.

"Good." She lingers and something passes between us—sister, ally, threat, all braided so tightly I can't tell which strand is thicker or if they're all the same.

Behind her, Lucinda stands at the desk, hands flat on either side of a legal pad, smile wide and white, like they were having a sentimental heart-to-heart and not a verbal knife fight.

Zoey leans in until her breath warms the cup of my ear.

"Don't leave," she whispers. "Not yet. Please."

"Why not?" I whisper back, throat tight.

"Because I need a witness," she says. "And you're the only one still living."

She pulls back and checks my eyes like she's checking a lock, then she brushes past me into the hall, a stormfront in a sweatshirt.

The lamp light from the study spills across my feet before Lucinda finally flicks the switch. I tiptoe around the corner, lurking in a dark hallway before she steps out into the foyer.

The door clicks shut behind her.

Footsteps climb the staircase, slow and methodical.

The house holds its breath.

And so do I.

44

I wait for Lucinda to disappear into her room before heading upstairs. The second I round the corner, Zoey stops me, her cheeks still flushed from her exchange with Lucinda, her eyes wide with something that resembles calculation. She grips my wrist and pulls me into her bedroom, shutting the door with an inaudible click.

"I need to tell you everything, and I swear to you, every word is true. You don't have to believe me. I know that. But at least hear me out." Her voice is steady, but her hands tremble. Half of me believes her, the other half of me knows she could be playing me like a fiddle. Like she said before . . . *everyone lies here.* "Lucinda told me if I helped poison my dad, I'd get a third of the estate. Eleven million dollars. Evan was supposed to get the other third. She said it would be easy. That the poison was undetectable. That if I gave it to him in tiny doses, it would be painless. She would stir it into his drinks and sprinkle it on his food. But I gave him candy. I told her it was laced . . . but that was a lie. I never poisoned him. I played along with her game because I knew there'd be consequences if I didn't."

My stomach tightens at how casually she speaks about sitting idly by while her mother and biological father plot the murder of an innocent person—a man who raised and loved her—but then I remember who and what she is.

"When he was at the hospital last time, I found his will," Zoey presses on, almost relieved to get it out. "It was updated six months ago and he left everything to me with a yearly stipend for Mom. We went to the estate lawyer today. I found out Dad changed the will right before he died. Just like you said. Left *everything* to her. Nothing for me. No provisions except some money for college and a car. I guess he assumed she'd make sure I was taken care of? He always bought into her bullshit. But she lied to me, Camille. She used me. I could've warned him. I should've warned him. But I was afraid of what she'd do to me, how she'd spin it. I mentioned it once last year and she threatened to send me away to this horrible place for bad kids. She was going to kill him regardless. I couldn't stop her. I knew if I went away, he'd die even faster, if I stayed and kept my mouth shut, at least I'd have more time with him . . . I *hate* her."

I think back to the study, to Lucinda's flat, cold voice, to the way she snapped her daughter into silence.

I hated her, too.

In fact, all these years later, I don't know that that's changed—it's only lost its power over me.

"Yesterday, at the police station," Zoey continues, "the detective asked me questions like he already knew the answers. Like he believed I had something to do with it. Mom keeps threatening to throw me under the bus, but I think she already did."

I recall overhearing Lucinda's interview. The way she carefully framed her answers, subtle but pointed, planting suspicion in the detective's mind. My pulse races. I know Zoey's right. But I also know when people like us feel cornered, we lash out. Rage is one of the few emotions we're able to feel, and when we feel it enough, it's never a good thing.

"She's grieving," I say, trying to soothe and not ignite her further. "She's not thinking clearly. You can't read too much into this right now."

I can't believe I'm defending Lucinda, but in this moment, Zoey's rage and teenage impulsivity have the potential to be a lethal combination . . . again. I need to calm her down before she does something rash and makes this worse for all of us.

She shakes her head hard. "You know damn well everything she does is intentional."

Without missing a beat, she pulls something from between her mattress and box spring and places it on the bed: a silver MacBook Pro. When she flips the lid open, the glow of the screen lights her face in ominous shades of midnight blue.

"This is her laptop," she says, proving it by typing in a password and pulling up synced text messages—Lucinda's number at the top. "See."

She scrolls through various texts, almost all of them from family and friends sympathizing over her loss, asking if she needs anything, letting her know they're dropping off a meal. Next she opens a web browser and pulls up Reddit. It's already logged into an account. My heart free-falls to the floor when Zoey clicks on the comment history.

It's all there.

All the posts that gave away our location . . .

Even the ones mentioning the children's disguises . . . which I wasn't aware she knew about . . . it's all there.

It was Lucinda the whole time.

"It gets worse," Zoey says, navigating back to Lucinda's texts. "Look." She turns the screen closer to me. "She's been texting Will since the day you got here."

LUCINDA: They're here. I'll let you know when you can come. Until then I'll take good care of them.

WILL: Don't let them leave under any conditions.

LUCINDA: I won't.

WILL: And send me updates daily.

LUCINDA: Of course.

LUCINDA: If this is going to work, you need the public—and your wife—to believe you're still looking for them.

WILL: I can do that.

I scroll through their conversations, which are chock-full of updates and sneakily captured photos of the children—clearly taken without any of us realizing. Lucinda's online posts giving away our location makes sense now . . . she wanted me to feel trapped, like he was closing in on me, like this mansion prison was our only refuge from the approaching storm. She orchestrated all of it—perfectly.

My flesh is so hot it leaves me dizzy.

I want to scream.

I clamp a hand over my mouth to keep from yelling the string of profanities trying to force their way out.

"She's an evil bitch." Zoey slams the laptop shut. "She never cared about you. She told me you two always hated each other, that you tried to kill her fourteen years ago. This is her chance to punish you."

"Jesus," I mutter under my breath.

It's all a game to her. Always has been.

I think back—Lucinda's sudden sweetness, her insistence that I not leave, her smothering hospitality. All the things that didn't make sense make perfect sense now.

It wasn't just a performance, it was a trap.

She knew I was in danger, that I needed her help. She lured me in with kindness and the facade of protection—all along knowing she was planning to feed me to the very wolf who'd been hunting me.

Zoey leans close, her eyes bright, fevered. "We have to take her down. And your husband, too. He's on his way here."

I'm paralyzed, heart pounding. I don't know if I can trust Zoey. She could be manipulating me so I help her take Lucinda down—but the texts and evidence on Lucinda's laptop are damning.

"I'm sorry," I whisper. "But if Will's going to be here soon, the kids and I have to leave. *Immediately.* We don't have a choice."

Zoey's still talking, her mouth sharp and fast, but I'm already moving, trailing downstairs like our lives depend on it because they do. I gather my kids' things—Mr. Red, blankets, crayons shoved into backpacks. Then I head upstairs where they're playing quietly in our room.

"Kids, we're leaving. Now," I say. They don't ask questions. I'm sure they hear the urgency in my voice and can see it in the snap of my movements. We head downstairs with all of our things in tow.

Zoey shadows me, relentless energy spilling off her in waves. "You're making a mistake."

I ignore her and force my focus on wedging tight sneakers onto little feet.

I shove my phone in my pocket and feel for my car keys—they must be upstairs.

The second floor might as well be a foreign destination at this point.

I sprint up and find them on the nightstand. I snatch them before feeling for the hunting knife, which I've been keeping under my bra 24/7 lately. By the time I return downstairs, I'm met with Lucinda in the kitchen, humming, spreading peanut butter and jelly on bread for my kids who are seated like two perfect little cherubs at the kitchen island.

"Hope you don't mind," Lucinda says in a singsong voice. When did she leave her room? Did I make too much noise running back and forth? I tried to be swift but silent. "The kids said they were hungry."

I press my keys hard into the palm of my hand, keeping them hidden. "Oh, you didn't have to do that, but thank you so much."

She's humming a haunting song, vaguely familiar, no lyrics. Just a creepy lullaby sung by a real-life monster. It's a tune I've heard a hundred times before and now she's performing it in front of my sweet children to taunt me.

A minute later, she stops and glances over, butter knife pointed at me. "What was with all the commotion a little while ago? Was someone running?"

Zoey and I exchange looks and play dumb.

For whatever reason, Lucinda lets it go.

I hold my breath, waiting for her to ask why all their toys and bags are next to the garage entrance, but now I'm thinking she hasn't seen them yet.

"Kids, after you eat, I thought the three of us could go out for ice cream." I get them excited on purpose. Georgie and Jackson love ice cream more than Disneyland.

"That sounds lovely." She plates their sandwiches, cutting the crust off with surgical precision like some domestic goddess. "There's a great local shop up the road in the Old District called the Sundae Parlor. They always have fun flavors, all made in-house. Zoey loves going there, don't you, Zoey?"

Zoey nods, playing along.

"Mind if we tag along?" Lucinda bats her lashes.

Zoey gives me a silent warning in the form of a side-eyed glance.

"It's a little pricey being artisanal and all," Lucinda adds, brows lifted. "My treat, of course. I know things are a little . . . tight right now."

Message received loud and clear.

She's not letting us go anywhere without her.

And she won't let us leave this easily.

The kids shovel their sandwiches down their throats in record time, debating ice cream flavors between sticky bites.

Once they're done, I herd them toward the garage door, kicking their bags into the laundry room before Lucinda notices them. In the meantime, she grabs her purse off the kitchen counter and jangles her car keys with a mile-wide grin on her face—a look of pure satisfaction, control, and power.

"I'll drive," she announces, pausing to retrieve her phone and type out a text message. "Come on, Zoey. Get your shoes on."

I think of her texts with Will.

For all I know, she could be taking us straight to him.

"Actually, if it's okay with you, I'd like to drive. My car's been sitting idle for a while. Probably needs to be driven. I want to make sure the battery doesn't die or something. You know how old cars can get sometimes."

Lucinda hesitates, lips bunched at one side, then she shrugs. "All right."

Somehow we pass the laundry room without Lucinda noticing our bags—or if she did notice, she pretends not to.

A minute later, my hands are at ten and two on the steering wheel, palms damp as everyone buckles up. I hit the garage door opener.

For now, we'll get fancy ice cream. But tonight? We're gone.

Shifting into reverse, I begin backing up—only to be met with the crunching sound of my bumper scraping someone else's.

I didn't see a car there before . . .

Glancing in the rearview, I spot a black sedan parked behind my garage stall. The driver's door opens, unhurried and methodical, and within seconds, out steps a broad-shouldered, brown-haired, blue-eyed man I know too well.

"Daddy!" Jackson and Georgiana scream in unified joy, scrambling to get out of the back seat before I can stop them.

Shit, shit, shit.

I've imagined this scenario before—Will showing up. I've practiced how I'd respond in my head a hundred times. But none of those scenarios, none of my perseverating prepared me for a reunion like this.

Zoey meets my eyes in the rearview, giving off a silent "I told you so."

Lucinda wears the mask of manufactured confusion, like she didn't puppet master this whole thing.

"You," I say between gritted teeth. "You did this."

I don't give her time to respond before climbing out of the car, slamming the door, and marching over to my estranged husband, who now has a kid hoisted in each arm.

"Camille, hi." At first take, he looks and sounds like the kind family man I thought I married. He fooled me once. I'll be damned if he fools me again. I waste no time retrieving the children out of his arms. "I've been looking for you for weeks. I was worried something bad happened."

The only bad thing that happened to us . . . was him.

"Mommy said you had to work," Jackson says.

Will's eyes haven't left mine yet. They're all but boring into me, laser sharp, the kind of intensity that would make a normal person cower.

But there's nothing normal about me.

"This must be my son-in-law, Will." Lucinda approaches him with an outstretched hand and a graceful smile fit for a beauty pageant contestant. "Welcome, welcome. It's so wonderful to finally meet you. Why don't you come inside? We can all sit down, get to know each other, maybe have a nice chat."

A nice chat . . .

Whatever plan Lucinda's been scheming is officially in full swing, and there's not a damn thing I can do to stop it.

Not yet.

But I will.

I grip my children's hands with superhuman strength as we all head inside. I'm not letting go of them, not for one second.

It occurs to me as we walk inside that I know exactly how I need to handle this—even if it makes me die a little on the inside.

45

I wait until Lucinda is prepping iced tea in the kitchen, all charm and porcelain, and Zoey is occupying the kids in the living room before taking Will by the hand and leading him down a hallway. The move startles him at first, but he interlaces his fingers with mine.

"Thank God you're here." I throw my arms around his shoulders and bury my face in his neck, dragging in an exaggerated breath.

He's quiet, as if he's not quite sure how to respond. This wasn't the reaction he was expecting, I know, and that's the whole point.

"I made a mistake." I peer up into his eyes. "I never should've left. I never should've come here. I never should've trusted her."

I keep my voice hushed and my words frantic.

Will cups my face, his hands tender like they used to be before he showed his true colors and our life went up in flames.

"What's going on?" he whispers. He looks tired, unshaven, and still handsome in that too-perfect way that fools everyone but me. There's a storm brewing outside that makes the whole scene cinematic: thunder rolling in the distance, rain beading at the windows, and house full of people who've been playing God for far too long. "Camille." He says my name like a prayer. "Talk to me."

I inhale softly, blink tears that aren't real. "You scared me. Back in Phoenix. That wasn't the man I married. I . . . I thought we were in danger. I didn't have anywhere to go. I didn't want to come here, but it was the only place I thought you might not look for us."

I let tears spring in my eyes. He knows what I am. He knows how I work. But regardless, I'm his prized possession and he still wants me, which means he's desperate to believe this is real, that we can go back to the way it was before.

"She won't let us leave," I tell him. "I've been trying for weeks. She's cut off all my communication with the outside world. I have no money. She locks the house at night. There are cameras everywhere . . ."

"Shh, shh, shh." He strokes his soft hands against my cheek. "You guys are leaving tonight. With me."

"You don't understand how she works . . ."

"She invited me here, she told me you just needed time to cool off, that she wanted to help us be a family again."

Idiot.

"She lies," I tell him. "Everything that comes out of her mouth is a lie."

Which is ironically the truth.

"I wanted to call you," I whisper. "So many times. I wanted to come home. But she"—I glance toward the stairs where Lucinda disappeared, my voice breaking—"she wouldn't let me."

His eyes sharpen, then soften, like all the anger he'd been bottling for me has suddenly directed itself to her.

It's working.

"She said she'd take the kids if I left. She took my phone. Cut me off from everyone. Said she'd tell the police I was unstable. Will, I didn't know what to do." I beat my fist against his chest, soft, though, and bury my head once more. "I just wanted *you.*"

He wraps me in his arms, squeezing me tight like he's some savior, like he didn't blackmail me and all but keep me prisoner in our own home not that long ago. That protective instinct of his—the same one that made him dangerous—is alive and well.

"You're safe now."

"It's not that simple." My voice shakes on command. "You don't know what she's capable of. She's been controlling me since I was a kid. I thought I could protect the children by staying quiet, by doing everything she wanted, but she found ways to twist everything."

Will exhales through his nose. "I knew it. I knew something was off about her."

No shit.

I touch his hand, gently, long enough to make him remember what it felt like when I used to make him feel loved. "You were right about so many things. You were just protecting our family, keeping us together. I wish I'd listened. Instead she's been keeping us here like prisoners. She won't even let the kids leave the backyard. Half the time she won't let them out of the house."

It's a lie I know will grind his gears in the worst way. And it does. His jaw clenches.

All this time he thought I was the one keeping his kids from him—and technically I was—but now he thinks it was Lucinda.

"Your hair." He runs his fingers through my chopped pieces.

"She made me do it. Said it would make it harder for you to find me."

"Why would she say that when she told me exactly where you were?"

I force my lips to tremble. "She's crazy. I've told you. You know this. She's . . ."

I let my voice trail so he can fill in the blanks with whatever worst-case scenario he wants to imagine.

"I'll handle her." He swallows, determined. "And then I'm taking you and the kids home."

"You don't know how dangerous she is." My voice breaks again, practiced and perfect, though I speak the truth. "If anything happens to me—promise the kids will be okay."

"Nothing's going to happen to you," he says, voice dark with promise. "Or the kids."

If he can get us out of here, surely I can find a way to get away from him. I've done it once. I can do it again. Even if it takes longer this time. Even if it means living with him, pretending we're happy again, and getting a part-time job so I can bank away some escape money all over again.

Whatever I have to do to get away from Lucinda—I'll do it.

"We better get to the living room," I say.

He squeezes my hand, giving me an offer of reassurance. At this point, Will is my best bet and only chance at freedom from Lucinda.

A moment later, when we're all seated, Lucinda returns with that Stepford smile and a tray full of iced tea in hobnail glasses. It occurs to me now that I haven't warned him about her—not enough.

She hands Will the first glass. He accepts it with a forced smile, gulping down over half of it. He must be back on that medication that makes him insatiably thirsty. That's the only time I see him drink that fast.

"Well isn't this just so nice?" she asks, once we're all settled and the silver serving tray is resting on her mirrored coffee table, nestled between family photos. "All of us, together, finally. The way it should be. The way it always should've been."

Will turns, slow and deliberate. "Actually, no, Lucinda. Camille told me everything."

I inhale a sharp gasp.

I didn't know he was going to go for her jugular immediately. I thought he understood we had to be strategic? Did I not instill enough fear in my delivery a moment ago? Were the tears and shaking not convincing enough? Or is he arrogant enough to believe he can conquer someone like her?

Lucinda's smile doesn't move, but her eyes do—a flicker of fury behind glass. "I'm sorry? What do you mean . . . *everything*?"

"How you kept her here against her will. How you isolated her. The way you treated the children."

"Will," she says smoothly, though her eyes drift to mine, "it sounds as if you've been terribly misinformed. Would you mind stepping into the next room with me?"

He follows her into the foyer, a move that could easily prove deadly if he's not careful.

"Don't gaslight me," he snaps. "I know all about you. You've been manipulating and controlling her since childhood. You promised to keep her safe, but all you did was hold my family hostage."

Lucinda laughs—a sound too light to be real.

"How was I holding them hostage, exactly?" Her fingertips trail her décolletage delicately, seductively almost. "I believe you and I were in contact from early on. I was keeping them here . . . specifically for you. Did I not make that clear?"

"She wanted to leave. She wanted to come home. You wouldn't let her." His words are terse, rage filled. "Do you have any idea what these past few weeks have been like for me?"

"Will." She tuts. "I'm afraid you don't know your wife as well as you think you do. She's gone to great lengths to stay hidden from you. Anything she tells you otherwise is a lie. She manipulates. That's what she does. That's what she's doing now. She wants you to think I'm some kind of villain, and I'm not sure why. She's always been a little . . . off."

The air between them crackles. Zoey and I exchange looks. We know exactly what she's doing and this could go a number of ways.

"I'm taking my family and we're leaving," he tells her.

"Of course," Lucinda counters. "That's the whole point of this visit, isn't it?"

Will is quiet, as if that wasn't the reaction he was expecting, like he thought he'd have to put up a fight.

Honestly . . . same.

"I don't imagine I'll get the opportunity to spend time with you and the grandkids again after this," she says in a way meant to arouse sympathy. "Please at least stay and visit? An hour is all I ask."

Silently, I think the words *no, no, no* over and over again, wishing against hope that the message will magically transmute to his mind.

This is a trap and he's walking right into it.

"One hour, then we're gone," he says.

Zoey's expression falls.

"Why are Daddy and Grandma talking so long?" Jackson whines.

"I think they're about done," I say, "but you can go check on them if you'd like."

His little face lights and he trots to the foyer, returning with both of them in tow.

When Will's back is to Lucinda's, she shoots me the nastiest look I've ever seen—something that suggests I've betrayed her in the worst way, that she isn't done with me, that she's already scheming on ways to make me pay for this.

As thunder rolls through, we make small talk. Surface level and superficial. Meaningless. Pointless. With each passing minute, Will's eyes grow droopier, his words are delivered slower, and every once in a while he slurs one of them.

Oh, God.

She drugged him.

46

"What's wrong with Daddy?" Georgiana asks, climbing into his lap. She cups her little hands on the sides of his face. "Daddy, why are you sleeping? Wake up."

Will is out cold, but at least he's still breathing.

This isn't good. Why does Lucinda need him sedated?

While the kids bounce on him, I give Lucinda a stern look. "What did you give him?"

She bites a sly smile. "An old family recipe. Couldn't risk him trying to sneak off with the kids in the night."

Zoey stares at the floor, silently keeping away everything she knows because now is not the time to spill anything.

"What did you give him?" I ask again, harder, before adding a lie, "He has a lot of allergies."

She sniffs and bats a flaccid wrist at me.

"Just a little something to help him relax. Whatever you told him had him really worked up. I wanted to make sure he wasn't going to do anything rash tonight," she says. "You can never trust an angry man."

And she would know.

She's pissed off more of them than she can count in her lifetime.

The kids climb off him, oblivious to our conversation, thank goodness.

"Why don't you help me get him to bed?" she says. "There's a guest room on the main level. He can sleep this off and we can all have a levelheaded discussion in the morning about where we're all going from here. Zoey, take the kids upstairs, will you?"

I can't tell if she's protecting me—or punishing me.

And asking is pointless. She'll never tell the truth.

As much as I detest Will and what he did to me back in Arizona, I hate to see him like this. Helpless. Drugged. But mostly, I hate to see him unable to help us escape.

"I think I should keep an eye on him," I say. "I have no idea what you gave him, and the last thing you need is another dead body in your house."

She swats away my suggestion. "Don't be so dramatic. He'll be fine by morning. Now help me get him down the hall. Zoey, you too. It's going to take all three of us."

"What are you doing?" the kids ask as they watch us hoist him over our shoulders.

"Your father drove a long ways," Lucinda lies to them. "He's very sleepy and needs to rest. You'll see him at breakfast, but for now, we're putting him to bed."

47

The world tilts before I open my eyes. Head is pounding. I squint at the spinning ceiling and the edges of the room melt into a hazy blur. It's like a hangover, only ten times more intense. I've never felt anything like this before.

Lucinda had to have drugged my iced tea last night.

That's the only explanation.

I took a sip from my glass without thinking. Just one. Whatever she laced it with had to have been potent.

I blink a few times, letting my vision clear, then I reach over for Jackson. The right side of the bed is empty. Springing upright, I turn to the left. No Georgie either. Flinging the covers off my legs, I realize there's far too much light creeping between the curtains. Grabbing my phone, I check the time: 9:47 AM.

I hurry to the hall then down the closest staircase, nearly losing my footing when I reach the bottom. Every step slower than I want it to be. My limbs are heavy and they don't feel like mine.

The house is quiet.

Too quiet.

I stumble to Will's room first, twisting the doorknob with a breath held so tight in my chest it burns.

The bed is made—but empty.

As if he was never here at all.

Turning around, I'm met with a bed-headed Zoey yawning and stretching her hands over her head.

"What are you doing?" she asks.

"Have you seen the kids?" My words come rushed, hurried, there's no time to inject gentleness or worry about the way I'm coming across. "Where's Will? And Lucinda?"

Zoey shrugs as if the question isn't a matter of life or death. I can't be sure if this is an act or if she just rolled out of bed and is genuinely clueless. For all I know, Lucinda drugged all of us. Regardless, in my current state, I want to grab her by the shoulders and shake the truth out of her.

The sound of giggles fills the empty space between us.

"Oh, my God," I mutter before following the sound, which might as well be music to my ears. I steady myself against the wall for balance, heading to the kitchen where I see two empty cereal bowls on the island counter.

The laughter is coming from outside, but they're not in the pool.

I jerk the sliding door open and find them chasing each other around an open section of yard, playing some made-up game and giggling like crazy.

"Jackson. Georgiana." I cross my arms. I'm furious—not at them so much but at the lack of control over my circumstances, at Will's arrival, at Lucinda's scheming—and I don't have the mental bandwidth to tamp that down. "Why did you come out here alone? Without me? You know you're not supposed to do that."

The giggles and chasing stop cold.

They turn to me, sheepish.

"We tried to wake you up, Mommy," Jack says. "But you wouldn't get up."

Georgie looks at me, slightly nodding. "We came downstairs and couldn't find anyone, so we made some cereal and went outside."

Oh, God.

Will and Lucinda are gone—together.

No possible good can come from the two of them together.

"Come inside," I tell them, motioning. *Now.*

They obey without question, though Georgie pouts and mutters a quiet, "Sorry, Mommy" as she passes.

"You two aren't allowed to go anywhere without me," I remind them. "We've talked about this."

Zoey's in the pantry, rummaging through boxes of cereal and granola, taking her time making herself breakfast.

"Did you see anyone this morning? Daddy or Grandma?" I ask the kids—this time sweetly. I think they're afraid of me at the moment, and I can't blame them. This is not the version they're used to. Panicked, angry.

Georgie shakes her head.

I shuffle to the front door, peering out the sidelight window to the driveway. Will's black Audi is missing.

Where would they have gone? And what would they be doing? And what's going to happen when they come back?

That's when it hits me—on my old phone, I had an app through my insurance company. They gave us a 10 percent discount on our premiums if we agreed to keep tracking devices in our cars. They said it was for safe driving, but I imagine it had more to do with preventing insurance fraud. Regardless, if Will still has his, I might be able to find him.

Pulling out my phone, I download the insurance app.

It takes less than a minute, but even that minute feels like a lifetime.

Within seconds, I'm logged in. I tap on "locate vehicles," then select the Audi. A spinning wheel and a caption below says, "Please be patient while we pull up your car's location."

I can't breathe.

This could be my only chance to find—the screen populates with a map and a tiny red dot.

I've located them . . .

. . . and they're at a state park thirty miles from here.

"Zoey, I need you to stay with the kids," I say. I hate leaving them under any circumstances, but I don't have a choice.

If Lucinda and Will were conspiring together, they'd surely do it via text or hushed conversations. But they didn't. Will berated her last night and she drugged him. The fact that she got him out of the house, away from his children, and alone?

I can still hear the venom in his voice. The way he spoke to her, he might as well have been signing his death warrant.

She's going to kill him.

And while I'd love for him to be a problem I no longer have to deal with, he was my ticket to freedom from this house, from *her*.

A chill crawls up my spine, settling between my shoulder blades. Maybe I'm being paranoid. Maybe I'm wrong. But I don't think I am.

"Kids, I have to go, but I'll be back. You're not to leave the house. Stay with Zoey. Don't open the door for anyone." My pulse is a drum line in my ears.

I collect my keys and go to slide my phone in my back pocket, only to remember I'm still wearing pajamas. But that's the least of my concerns because there's a very real chance I'm walking into a trap—and there's also a very real chance my mother is about to murder the father of my children and make an already complicated situation a hundred times worse.

"Mommy, you're scaring us," Georgie says, blinking up at me through her long, dark lashes.

I take a moment to hug her tight and kiss the top of her head.

I do the same to my son.

Then I leave.

The door clicks shut behind me, and for a moment, I can't tell if I left them safe . . . or abandoned them to a fate that I, for once, can't control.

If I drive fast enough, maybe I'll get there before it's too late.

48

The road to the state park is all hairpin turns and blind corners, the kind that make your stomach twist with every curve. My pulse hasn't slowed since I left the driveway. Pines blur past my window, the world still hazy from whatever Lucinda gave me last night, but I'm pushing through.

The elevation changes. Fewer fields and winding roads and more bluffs and cliffs and lakes—ideal terrain for hiding a body.

The GPS app on my phone notifies me I'm close, that the next turn is in three hundred feet on the right. Ahead, asphalt turns onto gravel. I pull onto a rock-covered road, past a sign that says No Trespassing.

Slamming on my brakes, I come to a hard stop when I realize something else: What if this setup wasn't to kill Will? What if it was meant to lure me out here so they could kill *me*?

I pound a fist against the steering wheel but it does nothing to satisfy. My limbs are heavy and my thoughts are molasses. It's hard to move with this drug in my system, but it's even harder to think. I chew my inner lip, debating whether or not to take this potential bait. Before I can decide, a sharp crack splits the silence.

A gunshot rings out.

Loud.

Unmistakable.

Echoing.

Instinct takes over. I slam the gas and continue up the gravel lane, overgrown tree branches smacking the sides of my car as I drive faster, faster still, before spotting Will's parked Audi glinting at the top of the lane, overlooking a cliff barricaded by a dented, broken barrier.

I shift into park and dash out of my car, leaving the driver's door open and sprinting toward her. My shoes slip on the gravel, but I don't stop.

From here, I don't see Will, only Lucinda with a gun pointed straight up in the air.

She fires another shot, and this time I'm so close it sends a painful ring to my ears.

I pick up my pace, the bottoms of my shoes scuffing as I shuffle closer. She doesn't notice me—or she's pretending not to. If I call out, I risk her pointing the pistol at me. And without knowing where Will is, if he's on my side, or if this is a setup, announcing my presence comes with risks—and my thoughts are too muddy to calculate those.

I trot another ten or fifteen feet when I see him. Will. The top of his dark brown hair, the flecks of salt and pepper at his temples that I used to think made him look wise and safe and fatherly. In a flicker of a second, I fixate on the version of him I appreciated until his true colors came out.

We'll never get back to that.

Or to *us*.

But at least he's still alive.

I open my mouth to speak, not yet sure what I'm going to say—but before I get a chance to collect my slow-motion thoughts, Lucinda lowers the weapon, points it at his head, and pulls the trigger.

The burn of bile rises up the back of my throat.

I fall to my knees, not wanting to believe my own eyes.

She killed him.

She actually killed him.

Lucinda tosses the small black handgun over the cliff. It catches the light before disappearing into the abyss like a secret being buried alive. She snaps a pair of gloves off her delicate hands with rehearsed precision, then spins around with calculated calm. When she notices me, she doesn't act surprised.

In fact, she *smiles*.

It's the kind of smile that isn't a greeting, the kind that implies *I've been expecting you.*

My instinct is to run—but this time I refuse. She *wants* me to be afraid of her. That's where her power lives. That's how she wins.

"Oh good. I'm glad you're here because I need your help." Her tone is smug, almost playful.

"Why?" I ask, breathless.

"Because he was a problem." She doesn't fight the pleased smirk taking over half her mouth. "Which is why I need your help."

"I'm not helping you. I want to know why you thought *this* was the solution?"

"There's no time for questions." She walks back toward the edge of the cliff, where she tossed the gun a minute ago. "I need you to help me move him. We have to be quick and then we have to get out of here."

My shoes are frozen to the ground as I stare at Will's lifeless body.

I attempt to swallow but my throat feels swollen.

I won't miss him.

But our children will.

There's a clean hole the size of a bullet in his temple, blood leaking out in scarlet rivulets that contrast with his bright blue eyes that are still wide open, frozen in place after his last breath. Even in death, the man is a sight for sore eyes.

I should look away, but I don't.

I can't.

I wait for horror that never comes.

Maybe that's what peace feels like? Nothingness.

Funny how someone can have everything—a loving, loyal wife, two beautiful children, the career of their dreams, a comfortable house in the suburbs—and throw it all away because of their ego.

If he were a good man, if he was the person I thought he would be, I imagine I wouldn't feel so numb staring at his dead body.

"Help me push him over the cliff." Lucinda is crouched down, cutting the zip ties from his wrists with something she grabbed from her pocket. "It has to look like a suicide."

To the left, there's a white envelope weighted down with a large gray rock. The words "to my wife and kids" are scrawled across the front in Will's barely legible but familiar handwriting. How she got him to do any of this is beyond me . . . but this is Lucinda's wheelhouse.

Manipulating men is what she does best.

"I don't think you realize, Camille, but it's only a matter of time before the DNR or a local officer shows up after reporting gunshots. We can't be here when that happens unless you want to spend the rest of your life in prison and I don't think . . ." She lets her sentence trail so I'll fill in the rest with worst-case scenarios. "Just get over here and help me."

I crouch beside her and place my hands on his still-warm body, a body that used to massage my feet and bring me coffee on Sunday mornings, a body that held my hand through two unmedicated births, a body that, once upon a time, belonged to a man who made me feel like life didn't have to be so bad after all.

Now's not the time to get nostalgic or to mourn a person who no longer exists, a person who really never did because it was all a mask.

Together, we roll him to the edge.

Once.

Twice.

On the third roll, his body slides down the rocky cliff, disappearing into the gorge below. It doesn't make as much sound as I thought it would. There's just a hollow stillness, broken only by a gust of wind rustling some nearby trees.

The dead silence that follows is terminal.

49

"Why?" I ask Lucinda when we're driving back to the house. "Why did you do this?"

"I think what you meant to say was *thank you for doing this*." She sniffs a laugh, like she's made some clever comment.

I grip the steering wheel harder to keep from clawing her eyes out, which is what I really want to do.

"I did you a favor." She clasps her hands in her lap, legs crossed at the knee. "A favor for the kids, too. And for us. We can finally be together again."

"You killed the father of my children," I remind her. "How can you call it a favor? I didn't need you to do that. I didn't ask you to do that."

"Evan tried to take you away from me and I didn't let that happen. I wasn't going to let Will do the same."

There's ownership in her voice. Possession disguised as motherly protection and devotion. She wants me under her control again. Dependent. Powerless. Forced to be grateful and bend to her every whim. Any money she gives me will only be an appetizer. A debt she'll make me repay one way or another. A power move, one that silently conveys Lucinda has a lot of money now, she's willing to share some with me, and if I need money again, I'll have to stay in her good graces.

"So killing him was the only solution?" I ask.

"No." She chuffs. "There were multiple solutions. This one just felt like the easiest." A few miles stretch on before she speaks again. "We don't need men, Camille. We never did. They're all just a means to an end. They give us babies. Sometimes they give us money or a lifestyle. But most of the time, they give us headaches. They're like needy children disguised as grown men. I've always found it a bit sordid how they want us to mother them. To make their meals and wash their clothes and shower them with love and affection. Beneath every grown man is an inner child who wants to be catered to."

"Maybe in your experience. They're not all that way."

Ironically she describes Will perfectly—in a way I'd never really thought about before because I did those things as his dutiful stay-at-home wife. Still, I know there are good men out there who aren't like this.

"Are you defending Will? After everything he did to you?"

"No." I start to add more, then stop myself. I don't have the energy to argue with her about this.

Reaching her hand across the console, she places it on my arm and gives it a loving squeeze.

"It's just going to be us from here on out," she says with a smile that—this time—reaches her eyes. "The way it was always meant to be."

I don't make space for her words in my mind. Instead I'm planning, plotting my next move.

Lucinda draws in a long, slow breath, releasing her grip on my arm. She lets it go with a gentle sigh. Seated beside me, she's somehow elegant, composed, and monstrous all at the same time.

While both Lucinda and Will were evil in their own ways, he was the lesser of the two.

"Funny, isn't it?" she muses aloud. "How peaceful life gets when your problems go away."

I couldn't agree more.

My life was pretty peaceful—until I let this monster out of her cage.

We say nothing the rest of the ride home, despite all the questions swirling in my head. How'd she convince him to go somewhere with her alone? How'd she bind his hands? How'd she force him to write a suicide note and what did it say?

I imagine she bound his hands when he was passed out from the drugs, maybe typed up a suicide note saying he was a lost, broken man and he lied about everything, that he was sorry to his wife and kids for what he put them through, that he couldn't go on knowing he was capable of doing the things he did.

Or maybe she lured him out here under the pretense of telling him I took off with the kids. That house is expansive and impossible to navigate unless you've been there long enough. She has a plethora of spare guest rooms. She easily could've shown him an empty one, got him worked up, then insisted they try and find us. If his mind was as groggy as mine was this morning, he wouldn't be thinking clearly enough to see through it—if he was even capable of seeing through it. This woman is as convincing as the snow is white.

Either way, I suppose it doesn't matter how she did it.

What's done is done.

We can't go back now.

"What am I going to tell the kids?" I ask her when we pull into the driveway. "You've really created a mess here. He didn't have to die for you and me to have a relationship."

She'll likely see through my guilt trip, but I don't care. I've got a mess to clean up, an escape to plan, and that's what I need to focus on.

"He didn't deserve you. Or the kids." She smooths her hair again and clasps her hands in prayer formation, still playing the role of Country Club Lucinda—reformed, benevolent, and beloved by others. "But me? I deserve a second chance, and just when I finally got one that waste of space was going to take it away."

This is a dangerous woman.

Who's to say she won't target my kids next? She's killed two people and ordered the execution of a third . . .

All within a matter of weeks . . .

And all for *me*.

We're leaving tomorrow.

Lucinda is—and always has been—a deranged, unhinged monster that destroys everything and everyone around her.

50

Lucinda wakes us before dawn with the smell of bacon, cinnamon pancakes, and strong coffee. By the time I drag myself downstairs with the kids, the dining room looks like a magazine spread—china, silverware, a tower of fruit skewers arranged like a centerpiece. She's in pearls again, hair set. I'm not certain she's slept at all. There isn't enough makeup in the world to cover the bags under her eyes this morning.

"Enjoy," she says, cheerful and commanding at once.

Jackson shovels scrambled eggs into his mouth.

Georgie stacks strawberries on toast like tiny red jewels.

Even Zoey plays along, buttering a pancake with a steady hand, her expression a mask. For half an hour, it almost feels ordinary, like maybe we've stepped into some alternate timeline where Lucinda is just a grandmother feeding her family.

Last night, after the kids went to sleep, Zoey cornered me and demanded to know what happened. Depleted and exhausted and planning to leave anyway, I told her everything I knew and as I expected, got no reaction. It was as if I told her her mom went to yoga. It meant nothing. There was no shock, no surprise, no gasp. Just a barely audible "Hm."

Then she went to her room and shut the door.

Jackson's asking for seconds and Lucinda's serving him like he's some little prince when a loud knock at the door comes.

Heavy. Aggressive.

Lucinda wipes her hands on a linen napkin, rises, and flits to the foyer like she's expecting company or another gigantic floral arrangement.

I get up, peeking out from a dark hallway, where I see two police officers.

Their voices are too far away to hear, but within minutes she's in the center of the two-story entry, beneath an oversized crystal chandelier, wrists pinned behind her back with cold steel ratcheted tight.

"Lucinda McClindon, you're under arrest for the murder of Robert McClindon. You have the right to remain silent . . ."

The words hang in the air like smoke. Everything is frozen in time for a moment.

I can't believe this is actually happening.

Instantly, Lucinda's calm shatters, her mask fading in real time.

Zoey and the kids join me in the hallway after following the sound of the commotion.

"What's going on? Why is Grandma being handcuffed?" Georgie asks.

Jackson clings to my leg. I don't like that they're seeing this. Their father is dead and the grandmother who has been nothing but (outwardly) adoring to them this entire confusing time here is being taken away by uniformed officers. But there's no shielding them from this.

My only consolation is their age. One day this'll be a distant memory. A hazy dream. If we're all lucky, maybe they'll forget it altogether, or if they do remember anything, it'll be that their mother stayed calm and composed and never left their side. Perhaps they'll remember they didn't have to go through something hard . . . alone.

"This is absurd!" Her eyes are blazing, her ears are cherry red, but her voice doesn't shake. She's performing, even now. "I didn't kill him. I didn't! Call my attorney. Tom Stuart. Call him *now*."

She doesn't look at Zoey. Only me. And her stare is accusatory, menacing.

Zoey doesn't move. She doesn't even blink. She stands there like nothing's happening. There isn't even a glint of satisfaction in her dead ocean eyes. She reminds me of myself before I learned to fake it. I've seen her fake her feelings before. I know she's capable. But maybe there's nothing to fake because she isn't sad to see our mother hauled away by the police, and feigning joy would require too much energy . . . and we're all exhausted.

It all happens in a vacuum. Breakfast. The knock. Lucinda being arrested.

And now she's gone.

Somewhere deep inside me, something exhales and a lightness washes over me, the kind that follows after years of holding your breath, looking over your shoulder, and carrying a weight that someone else placed on your shoulders.

The sirens don't turn on until they're halfway down the street, a courtesy, a silent mercy she doesn't deserve.

The quiet that follows feels ceremonial.

There's a finality in the air, like the closing of a book after the final page.

"Did Grandma get in trouble?" Georgie asks once the commotion is over.

"I'm not sure," I tell her because I don't know how to explain . . . any of this. Yet. "I'm positive we'll know more eventually. I'm sorry you had to see that, but *we* are going to be okay and that's the only thing you need to know right now."

With Lucinda gone, the house is calmer than ever. The kids watch cartoons on the sofa with full bellies, drained by the morning spectacle. After a while, I scour the house for Zoey, finding her in the study hunched over a laptop, clicking one of her father's favorite pens and staring blankly ahead.

She doesn't look up when I step inside.

There's something especially eerie about her stillness this time, though I have to wonder if being unreadable is a skill she had to master in order to survive under these conditions.

"Care to explain what just happened?" I fold my arms.

"Sure." She shuts the laptop lid and leans back, making herself comfortable in her late father's oversized desk chair. "The day she made me go in for questioning without an attorney? I brought everything with me. All the evidence I'd been compiling. Years' worth. My AirPods? Those double as listening devices and I found an app that turns them into recording devices, too. I also rigged the security cameras so they'd record everything and back up to cloud storage, so whatever Evan thought he deleted was never actually deleted. Photos of her and Evan, recordings of their conversations, stills of Lucinda mixing powder into my father's drinks. I documented everything and gave them all copies on thumb drives." She cocks her head, satisfied. "I compiled a mountain of evidence so high she'll never be able to climb out."

The room feels colder, sending a chill through me that prickles my skin.

If this is true, color me impressed.

Though now I'm wondering what else she's capable of.

"Guess all those true crime podcasts paid off," she snickers.

"Wait," I say. "Why'd you do it?"

I search her face for cracks. There aren't any.

After a bout of silence she finally sighs. "I did it for us."

51

Lucinda Nichols McClindon, once the glossy hostess of Willow Glen Country Club's charity luncheons, the woman who could command a room with nothing more than the arch of her brows and a velvet laugh, now wears state-issued khaki and eats her meals off a plastic tray. It's the kind of detail that would make most people feel pity.

I feel nothing but the cold satisfaction of balance restored.

Some people might call it karma.

Word trickles back to me in written letters and short phone calls that I take only because of the validation it gives me: She hates the food. The vegetables are mush. She despises the communal showers, and she refuses to touch the soap bars. The "perverted" guards watch her so she covers herself in paper towels. It sounds like she still tries to hold court, tries to charm the other women, but it doesn't work in a place where every inmate has lived her own private war. No one cares how perfect her posture is or that she used to wear Chanel. To them, she's just another woman who thought she could outrun the law.

She's one of them now.

She always was.

It's surreal, sitting in that courtroom with Zoey beside me, her hair tucked behind her ears, her expression cool and unreadable. The judge speaks of responsibility, of duty, of the "honor" of stepping into this role for the sake of a child. With Rob's family gone—save for a seventy-eight-year-old sister in Texas—and Lucinda behind bars, I'm Zoey's next of kin.

The gavel comes down fast: guardianship awarded to me.

Zoey's lawyer explains the stipend to me—an extremely generous six-figure yearly disbursement from the McClindon estate that will cover Zoey's living expenses until she turns eighteen. He says the numbers aloud, and they echo in my head like an answered prayer from a god I never knew was listening.

It's more than enough. Enough to put food on the table, to pay for school clothes, to keep the kids in sneakers that don't have holes in the toes. Enough to finally breathe without checking my bank balance. Enough to live. Enough, even, to invest for the future.

When the paperwork is signed, Zoey looks at me across the table, one corner of her mouth curved in that sly little smirk that makes her look just like her mother. But her eyes—they're not Lucinda's. They're sharper.

Later that night, after the kids are in bed, I sit her down.

"Moving forward, Zoey, we *have* to respect each other." I keep my tone measured. "This isn't optional. If you even think about crossing me—if you so much as *whisper* something sideways—I'll make sure you never see a dime when you turn eighteen. I'll drain every account. I'll call every lawyer. I'll burn it all to the ground. I'll take good care of you, but if this is going to work, I have to trust you."

In other words: Do something crazy and you'll be a ward of the state.

I just can't word it like that because that's exactly the kind of thing Lucinda would say and all it did was throw gasoline on the fire that was Zoey's defiance.

Zoey tilts her head, listening. There's no fear in her face, no teenage defiance either. Just calculation, like she's filing it away.

"I'm not trying to scare or threaten you," I say to Zoey. "I'm just telling you how it's going to be if I'm raising you. I'm not

Lucinda . . . but I am a product of her. Always keep that in the back of your mind."

Zoey smirks, her expression as cool as ice water. "Your kids are safe. That's all you need to know."

The words should comfort me, but they don't.

52

Over the weeks that follow, the kids all start school and the four of us meld into the strange rhythm of a new normal. The stipend comes through the first of the month, generously more than enough, and for the first time in forever, I buy groceries without scanning every barcode like it's a sin. The kids eat cereal from boxes with cartoon mascots, drink juice that actually tastes like fruit instead of powder, and eat freshly cut and peeled exotic fruits.

I'm meeting with a real estate agent later today to get this house listed. It's technically in the estate's name, so any proceeds will go to Zoey's trust. Once we sell it, we're going to move into something more manageable and with fewer bad vibes.

We *all* need a fresh start.

Zoey's been quiet lately. She doesn't laugh much, but she watches. Always. When Georgie struggles with her homework, Zoey's the one who slides onto the bench beside her, explaining fractions with eerie patience. When Jackson has a nightmare, Zoey's the one who sits on the edge of his bed, earbuds in her hand, quietly reassuring him that monsters aren't real.

But I know better.

Monsters are real.

They just don't always look like what you expect.

Sometimes they wear pearls.

Sometimes they call you their wife.

Sometimes they wear hoodies.

And yet—I can't deny it. She protects them. Fiercely, instinctively. Like they're the most important things in the world to her.

People like us can't feel love, not in the traditional sense, but what we feel is akin to a loyalty ten times more intense.

I'm hopeful Zoey's intense loyalty to my children is genuine, but only time will tell.

A couple of afternoons ago, I heard raised voices in the backyard. I stepped to the window and saw Georgie cornered by a neighbor girl, older, taller, her finger jabbing in Georgie's face. Before I could move, Zoey was there, positioning herself between them, shoulders squared, eyes cold.

She didn't touch the girl. Didn't need to. Her words were sharp enough.

"Say one more thing to her," Zoey said, her voice short and dangerous. "And I'll make sure you regret it for the rest of your life, you stupid little ugly rag doll."

The girl stammered, flushed, and bolted off.

I should've been horrified. I should correct her, tell her not to scare people like that. But instead I stood at the window, silent. Because I knew what I was seeing.

Zoey isn't good—not in the way people mean when they use the word.

But she's ours now.

And she's using her darkness for us, not against us.

So far.

Later, in the quiet of night, when the house hums with the sound of sleeping children, I lie awake thinking about Lucinda in her cell, Evan in his grave, and Will's decaying body lying on some cliff thirty miles from here.

This isn't the ending I imagined.

But maybe it's the one I needed.

And I've got Zoey—brilliant, terrifying Zoey—watching over us like a wolf in the shadows. Protecting us with her fierce loyalty because Lucinda took the ability to love out of her heart, the same way she did to me.

Zoey was Lucinda's creation, just as I was.

But she's mine now.

And I fully intend to show her how to use our "powers" for good.

53

Six months later

The moving boxes are unpacked and broken down, jammed into the recycling bin in the garage of the house I just rented with Zoey's stipend money. The brick mansion sold sooner than we expected—eight days on the market, full-priced offer, cash.

Zoey and I both agreed we needed a fresh start after everything. Between packing some nights, we'd search up different cities and imagine what life might be like in each one. It didn't take us long to land on Portland, Maine.

The ocean. The little islands. The history. The cobblestone streets. The houses untouched by time. It was different from Chicago, San Diego, and Phoenix in every way. But more than that, it seemed like the kind of place that felt a world away from everything, which was exactly what we were looking for.

For now, home is a rented two-story, four-bedroom 1940s Craftsman on a street where people wave but aren't nosy. Where neighbors chin-wag about property taxes, not affairs. The kids love their new school. Zoey too. She's fourteen now, a freshman at the local public high school. I've got an interview for a part-time job next week. For now, I don't need the job and I likely never will because I'm reinvesting most of the stipend money we don't use. I just need something to keep me busy while they're away during the day.

So far, Portland is pretty perfect.

The kids asked about Will a lot in the first few months after everything happened. I told them he had to go back to work, that I wasn't sure when we'd see him again. Then I held them, wiped their tears, and silently promised to make it up to them somehow.

They never knew his ugly side. They're allowed to miss him. In their minds, he was a loving father, and they don't deserve to have that notion ripped away from them.

I'm meeting a new therapist this afternoon. I need to unpack everything with someone capable of giving me objective, unbiased feedback. And I want someone to hold me accountable, so I can be the best version of myself at all times for these kids. Being a single mom of three now will inevitably come with stressful, impossibly difficult challenges at times. Maybe if I can feel a little earth beneath my feet, I'll be better equipped to handle those moments.

This morning, Zoey helped me hang curtains in the living room. Pale linen. Nothing fancy. She then asked if we could paint her room sage green—her favorite color. Apparently Lucinda forced her to keep her walls stark white at all times.

I'm done folding a few baskets of laundry when I head to the elementary school and pull into the pickup line. I'm a little early, so I check my email on my phone—not expecting the first one I see to be from Sozi, with the subject line reading interview request—tell all memoir.

How she can be writing a book when she can't even use proper punctuation is beyond me. I don't open it, but I don't delete it either. I imagine she wants my side, my insight, pieces of trauma in digestible quotes, but she'll get nothing. It's been six months. The world's already moved on and this case has been buried beneath fresher scandals and newer monsters—because that's the thing: There's no shortage of them in a world where everyone plays their own main character.

By the time her book hits shelves, no one will care about Will Prescott or what he did. They'll have forgotten our faces and our story.

And that's exactly how I want it.

54

Dr. Michelle Lanning's office smells like bergamot tea and compassion. Soft light filters through ivory blinds on her window, painting her pale yellow walls an even sunnier hue. A box of tissues is centered on a coffee table, strategically placed I'm sure—but I won't need it.

I never do.

I can't remember the last time I shed a tear.

Two hours pass with me spilling my life story, condensing it as much as possible as I couldn't possibly pack everything into two hours.

Dr. Lanning doesn't say much, she mostly listens and maintains a neutral, nonjudgmental expression.

"Camille, I'm going to be straight with you." When she finally speaks more than a few words, her voice is calm, tranquil, the kind that makes you wonder if she's even capable of raising it. "Your first clinician diagnosed you with sociopathy, but . . . I'm not entirely sure you fall on the antisocial personality spectrum."

I blink. Did she just say what I thought she said?

"So I've been misdiagnosed?" I ask.

Her lips curve slightly, in a kind way. It's a Lucinda-pleased-as-punch smirk.

"We're only human," she says. "And humans make mistakes. I need more time with you to be sure, but based on everything you've shared with me today, it's my professional opinion that the signs and symptoms you've been dealing with your entire adult life are a form of C-PTSD—or complex post-traumatic stress syndrome."

My brows knit as I ponder her words. I'd heard of C-PTSD before, but I'd never considered or looked into it. That Lucinda traumatized the humanness out of me was the story I always told myself because that's the story my first doctor told me. I think I was so desperate for an answer as to why I felt different—and she was an expert in the field—so I never questioned it.

"Intrusive thoughts, flashbacks, triggers, avoidance, isolation, insomnia, hypervigilance," she reads off her notes, continuing, "depersonalization, derealization, mood swings . . ."

She catalogs all the things I've felt the last fourteen-plus years dealing with it. Each word drags a thread through me, stitching something together that's starting to make sense.

"When you talk about not reacting to things the way you think a quote-unquote normal person would," she says, "perhaps you adopted that as a coping mechanism. You had to shut that off to survive. Or at least you thought you did. Growing up, you were never given a safe space to feel your feelings, so never learned how. You didn't let yourself get attached because the only thing you knew was that attachment equaled pain."

I study her bookcase, rows of spines with words like *healing* and *resilience* and *trauma recovery*.

"But I can't feel anything," I tell her. "I can't even feel love for my own children. I'd die to protect them, but I don't feel love the way other mothers do."

Her eyes squint and soften and she angles her head. "What do you think motherly love is supposed to feel like?"

"I wouldn't know."

"Exactly," she says. "How would you know what that kind of love feels like if you've never been loved that way? Or loved at all?"

She's not wrong. Lucinda didn't love me, and while Will acted like he loved me, I never truly felt it. Looking back, they were all hollow motions, like he was playing a character.

"You know," she continues, "everyone thinks love is a feeling, but it's really an action. A verb. A choice. Love isn't butterflies and giddiness—those come from bonding chemicals in our brain like oxytocin. Everything you've done to protect your children—how you sacrificed, planned, and survived? Those are all acts of love." Her mouth curls up at the sides. "Camille, you *love* them."

With those words, something inside me shifts. It's small. Like a spark, not a flood. Unfamiliar warmth sits low in my chest, like an engine resting after running hot for years.

For the first time in my life, I let myself exhale—fully.

Maybe Dr. Lanning is onto something.

EPILOGUE

ZOEY

Every house has rules. Some people make you take your shoes off at the door. Others don't allow food outside the kitchen. There are homes where bedtime is sacred, screens go dark after eight, and voices soften after ten.

And then there are homes like ours.

Small. Warm. Safe.

We have rules in this house, too. Like . . . tell the truth, even when it's hard. Say you're sorry and mean it, and don't pretend everything is fine when it isn't. If you need space, take it. If you need help, ask for it.

No one keeps secrets here.

No one whispers behind closed doors.

We keep the lights low at night because Camille has shown me that the dark isn't scary anymore, that it can be anything you want it to be because you decide what everything means to you. I've decided darkness means comfort. It doesn't make sense, but I wanted to test her advice and so far it's working.

The human brain is funny that way.

It believes whatever you tell it.

Camille's nothing like Lucinda. She doesn't try to control every move I make. She doesn't smile with knives behind her teeth. She's strict some-times, sure—she makes rules about phones, about curfews, about how I talk to her in front of the kids. But she's fair. And she's kind. I see it in the way she holds her kids, the way she notices the tiniest things, the way she'd burn the whole world to the ground before she'd let anyone touch them.

Sometimes at night I wonder why she even lets me stay, why she said yes to being my guardian. She didn't have to. But then I see the way she looks at me when she thinks I'm not watching. It's not pity. It's not fear. It's like she's deciding something. Like maybe she sees a piece of herself in me.

Maybe she's right.

For the first time in my life, the future feels bright. Not blindingly bright. But bright enough . . . because Lucinda can't touch me anymore. Evan's gone. And while my dad's gone, too, at least I don't have to watch him die a slow and painful death right in front of me.

Camille. Georgie. Little Jack-Jack. They're my family now.

If anyone tries to hurt them, they'll have to go through me first.

That's the part Lucinda never understood. She thought she was teaching me to be her little protégé, her shadow, her second act. What she really taught me was how to survive, how to watch, how to strike when it matters most.

And now, with her locked up for life, I get to choose when and how and on whom I use those teachings.

Camille was Lucinda's daughter.

I am, too.

Together, we're going to be an unstoppable force.

Oh, and the last and most important rule in this house? It's that love isn't something you say . . . it's something you do. If that's true, I'm pretty sure Camille loves me. She's teaching me how to drive so I can get my permit next year, she always does my laundry instead of dumping wrinkled piles of clothes on my bed, she listens to me vent about friend drama or annoying teachers at school, and every day she packs me a healthy lunch and includes handwritten notes that say things like, "Be kind, be brave, be you." They're cheesy, and sometimes I wish she'd stop because they're a little embarrassing, but I think that's her way of showing she loves me.

And that's fine, because I think I love her, too.

Author's Note

Dear Reader,

When I first started writing this trilogy, the plan for book three was to call it *Married Strangers*, and it was going to be centered around how well Camille knew Will. But after writing book two and the Lucinda story arc not yet concluding, I couldn't waste the opportunity to force Camille to demonstrate her strength by facing her real-life demon: Lucinda.

Throughout the first two books, Lucinda existed mainly off page via haunting memories, flashback scenes, and bizarre letters. As strange as it sounds, I felt bad putting Camille in such a vulnerable position—her literal worst nightmare—but I knew she could handle it, and I promised myself I'd give her the justice and freedom she always deserved.

By the time I reached the end of this series, I realized it wasn't simply about a "sociopathic suburban mom." It was about what it means to be human in all its messy and contradictory forms, about boiling us down to our basic need to survive and thrive, to feel safe and loved via any means necessary.

Whatever Camille's true diagnosis is, it doesn't take away from the fact that her character was only human, and that while we're all capable of good and evil, at the end of the day, what we choose is our choice.

If you've made it to the end of the series, thank you. And thank you for embracing my flawed characters, uncomfortable truths, and the notion that we can be broken and beautiful at the same time.

Yours,

Minka

ACKNOWLEDGMENTS

To my readers—thank you for showing up, book after book, with your theories, messages, empathy, and passion for my flawed and complicated characters. You're the reason I get to do what I love. Every download, every share, every post, every review, every recommendation means more than you know. It's because of you that my stories find their way into the hands of new readers, and I'm endlessly grateful for you.

To my editor at Thomas & Mercer, Jessica Tribble Wells—thank you for your trust, your vision, your patience, and your unwavering belief in this series. And to Charlotte Herscher, my brilliant developmental editor, thank you for helping me dig deeper, push harder, and find the heartbeat under the rubble. To the entire T&M team— thank you for all the behind-the-scenes magic that brings this book to life in ways I could never do alone.

To my agent, Jill Marsal—thank you for your guidance, your patience, and your fierce support over the years. I'm lucky to have you in my corner.

To Maxine, Leslie, Rachel, Lindsey, Pon, and Dida—thank you for being the kind of friends who both cheerlead and keep my sanity in check.

To my children—thank you for celebrating every milestone with me, for keeping me grounded and humble, and for reminding me that life is meant to be lived outside the writing cave (even if that means sprinting between a million activities in one day).

Lastly, thank you to Michael for making my world softer, brighter, and so full of peace that the words flow easier now than they ever have.

With love and gratitude,

Minka

Book Club Questions

1. The novel opens with the line: "The only thing more danger-ous than where I've been is where I'm going." How does this set the tone for the book? Did it match your expectations of where the story went?

2. What were your first impressions of Camille? Did they shift over the course of the series?

3. Camille disguises her children and teaches them to "play a game" in order to survive. How did this affect your perception of her as a mother? Does this strategy make her cruel, brilliant, or both?

4. What do you make of Evan? Did you trust him at any point? Why or why not?

5. Lucinda embodies a polished, Stepford-wife image but hides deep cruelty. What makes her such a chilling villain? Were you satisfied with her downfall?

6. Zoey is perhaps the most complex character—both victim and predator. Did you see her as a true ally to Camille, or simply another manipulator?

7. The book often blurs the line between "good" and "bad" mothers. Who do you think the most dangerous parent figure was, and why?

8. Gaslighting, manipulation, and surveillance recur throughout the novel. Which example stood out to you most and why?

9. Identity is a constant theme: the children are disguised, Lucinda has reinvented herself, Evan hides in plain sight, Will gives TV interviews as a worried father. What does the novel suggest about how identity can be weaponized?

10. Which twist shocked you the most? Did you see any of them coming, or were you caught off guard?

11. Camille becomes Zoey's guardian and accepts money from the estate. Did this feel like justice, irony, or a new kind of trap?

12. Do you think Camille and her children are truly safe with Zoey in the house? Why or why not?

13. If there were a follow-up, what would you want it to explore—Zoey's adulthood, Camille's attempt at normalcy, or the children growing up under their guardianship?

About the Author

Photo © 2024 Jill Austin

Minka Kent is the *Washington Post* and *Wall Street Journal* bestselling author of *After Dark, Gone Again, The Memory Watcher, People Like Them, The Perfect Roommate, The Silent Woman, The Stillwater Girls, The Thinnest Air, Unmissing, The Watcher Girl,* and *When I Was You,* as well as *Circle of Strangers* and *Imaginary Strangers* in the Dangerous Strangers series. Her work has been featured in *People* magazine and the *New York Post* and has been nominated for two International Thriller Awards, an Audie, and a Shirley Jackson Award. *Unmissing* was adapted for Lifetime in 2024. Minka also writes contemporary romance as *Wall Street Journal* and #1 Amazon Charts bestselling author Winter Renshaw. For more information, visit www.minkakent.com.